Other books by the author

Story Collections

Oldcat and Ms. Puss: A Book of Days for You and Me
The World's Thinnest Fat Man
Some Heroes, Some Heroines, Some Others

Editor

*Belles' Letters: Contemporary Fiction by Alabama Women (with
        Tina Jones)*
*Tartts One: Incisive Fiction by Emerging Writers (with
        Tina Jones)*
*Tartts Two: Incisive Fiction by Emerging Writers (with Tina Jones,
        Debbie Davis, and Gerald Jones)*
*Tartts Three: Incisive Fiction by Emerging Writers (with Tina Jones
        and Tricia Taylor)*
Tartts Four: Incisive Fiction by Emerging Writers (with Tricia Taylor)

Masques

for the

Fields of Time

Joe Taylor

Livingston Press
The University of West Alabama

Copyright © 2009 Joe Taylor
All rights reserved, including electronic text
isbn 13: 978-1-60489-033-4 library binding
isbn 13: 978-1-60489-034-1 trade paper
Library of Congress Control Number 2009900214
Printed on acid-free paper.
Printed in the United States of America,
Publishers Graphics
Hardcover binding by: Heckman Bindery

Typesetting and page layout: Joe Taylor
Proofreading: Margaret Walburn, Shelly Huth,
Stephen Slimp, Rolfe Tanner,
Tricia Taylor
Cover design and layout: Jennifer Brown & Gina Montarsi
Cover artwork: "Limulus Christus" WB Montgomery

Some stories were published in slightly different form in these magazines:
Apalachee Review, Lake Effect, Gihon River Review,
The Sucarnochee Review, Hayden's Ferry Review

Livingston Press is part of The University of West Alabama,
and thereby has non-profit status.
Donations are tax-deductible:
brothers and sisters, we need 'em.

first edition
6 5 4 3 3 2

Table of Contents

For Stephen Slimp,
Tricia Taylor,
and Heather Loper Walker,
each of whom uniquely influenced this collection.

Masques

for the

Fields of Time

Down on the Dance Floor

One-two, one-two . . . Jimmy swayed to music coming from the old-fashioned record player near the yellow-brown warehouse wall. When the needle hopped over a scratch, he miscounted the oversized bare light bulbs overhead and had to start over.

One-two-three, four-five-six . . . there were twelve bulbs in all. The two near the front door had moths circling them, much as the dancers were circling one another on the planking of the warehouse floor. Jimmy was at the dance because of his older babysitter, who had abandoned him to the care of her brother, who was two years younger than she was and four years older than Jimmy. Eighteen minus two is sixteen. Sixteen minus four is twelve. Twelve minus ten is two. The people danced in groups of twos and Jimmy stood by himself, as one.

Things always return.

Along the distant wall, across the oak floor, a lineup of girls sat on folding metal chairs. One caught his attention, so he walked toward her, escaping from his erstwhile chaperone, who was talking with another girl, nearly a woman or even a crone in Jimmy's eyes.

As Jimmy closed toward the lineup, he became confused upon seeing that they all wore rigid white masks, some with blooded, angled grins; some with blackened frowns curving like sharpened sickles; some with purple lips laid flat like premature twins mourned on a catafalque. Where was the girl who'd caught his attention? He thought she might be the shortest one who sat in the middle of the twenty or so masks, so he walked toward her. The girl stood obligingly to dance when he was within two steps, and his head involuntarily tilted to the rafters to see if a puppeteer's strings had given her a yank up from the chair. When he did spy movement atop a thick, dark beam, his own shoulder twitched, so he gazed back into the girl's mask, finding it consoling, for the start of a smile glowed on the hard white plastic.

The song that was playing was wretched country cornball, "The Red River Valley." Nonetheless, they clasped hands and danced. Her hands were warm, even sweaty. Or were his very own hands sweating? The country-bumpkin record popped; no doubt the needle was flecked with dust. Jimmy glanced toward the record player. A bent man in a white suit with matching white hair that blared outwards, as if his cranium had been statically charged by a Van de Graaf accelerator, was nodding along with the music. One-two-three, one-two-three. In a waltz rhythm, his head bobbed.

But however Jimmy and the girl danced, they came up with two-four time. From this valley they say . . . one-two, one-two . . . buckle my shoe. Jimmy looked away from the strange man with the humped Jewish nose to his partner. He confirmed that her mask had become frozen in a grin. That was nice, wasn't it? He moved his face as close to hers as he dared. Clack! He was surprised to find that he too wore a rigid mask. He tried twisting his lips experimentally: a grin, a frown, a snarl. The girl paid no mind. What, he wondered, did his own mask look like?

He started to ask her just that, but the song ended, and she slipped back to her chair. He'll miss her bright eyes and sweet grin, Jimmy sang of himself, like he was the cowpoke left behind in the Red River Valley and the masked girl had run off with a city slicker. He turned on his heels, twisting a colt about, and ambled toward his chaperone, glancing back once to ascertain where the girl with the frozen grin had sat. But already she was lost in the crowd of masks, or maybe she had started to dance with someone else, because another old country tune—something no one ever really danced to, with its sad violins and all—was playing. "On the

Wings of a Dove," that was the name of it. About prison and God and the most Holy Paraclete. Why would an old Jewish man play that? Jimmy had gotten it in his head that the guy must be Jewish because of the nose. But then he could be Harpo Marx. But then, Harpo was Jewish too, wasn't he?

A large industrial fan with blades as long as his chaperone's arm was vibrating in a metal box as tall as Jimmy. The box had no front cover, and a young boy, say seven or so, just beyond the age of reason, squatted like a Buddha to its immediate right. Jimmy lurched, for he envisioned the boy slapping his left hand into the rotating blades, fingers and flesh and blood being sprayed over the dancers and the floor. But it was just a vision.

One-two, one-two . . .

Someone tapped Jimmy's shoulder before he could reach his chaperone. He turned into the mask of a tall girl, a frown this time, garishly black, with a silvered tear in the corner of each eye. She extended her arms and he obliged her by dancing to the song about the snow-white dove, staring at her Adam's apple until he realized that she was gazing over his head, searching for someone. She was leading, and he followed clumsily, though he didn't step on her feet. In fact, it was the other way around.

"Sorry," he said, even though she'd stepped heel-first on his right foot.

She didn't respond, but shoved him backwards and to his left. Evidently she'd located whoever she was looking for, for she abandoned Jimmy, rather like a dove flapping off, to tap another girl on the shoulder. The girl shrugged off her dance cut, so she tapped her again, harder, almost a shoulder punch. Instead of a fight developing like Jimmy thought might, the second girl gave up her partner and grabbed Jimmy to dance. He supposed it was the influence of the song, about the snow-white dove sending its pure sweet love from high up above.

One-two, one-two. This girl and Jimmy couldn't break the rhythm either, though this surely was another waltz. For confirmation, he looked toward the old Jewish gentleman, but this girl was leading too, and had dragged him toward the front door and those moths popping against the light bulbs, so he had to crane his neck backward and could barely spot the old geezer. For all Jimmy knew, he could be nodding his head to a Kaddish, maybe out of respect for the Buddha boy's imminent death, for the kid was still bobbing in front of the open, rotating blades, more like fighter airplane propellers.

Jimmy heard a snicker and turned to see his friends by the door, moths circling their heads as if they too were oversized light bulbs. How did they get here, his friends, that is? They seemed to be without chaperones and were too young to be out alone on such a dark, mothy night. Then Jimmy saw them point at him. The song had changed, I must tell you, since Jimmy himself was too worried over their snickering to be conscious of music. Though this new song was a fast one, the girl leading him gripped his shoulders and pulled him to her just-forming breasts, insisting that they—he, she, and the breasts—maintain the same one-two slow rhythm. But missed timing wasn't what his friends were laughing at. No, he realized with embarrassment, they were laughing because he had an erection. He could feel it pushing upward, nudging his waistline. New to this phenomenon, he worried, *Will it peep from under my shirt like a mouse?*

There was a slap of wood hitting wood. Two men, both with black moustaches, nineteenth century affairs, were carrying a ladder toward him and his partner. It was a 16-foot wooden monstrosity, which they extended around Jimmy and his partner as they circled in the bosomy clasp the girl insisted upon. Jimmy squinched his shoulders to avoid the ladder's wooden struts, and gazing between the ladder's paint-spattered steps, he looked for his friends, but the doorway loomed empty. Only night gaped inward, exhaling more moths. And his new chaperone, his babysitter's brother? Where was he as this girl-woman tugged at his shirttail? Was this girl-woman trying to make her last partner jealous by this close, almost dirty dancing? And just where were this girl-woman's ex-partner and the second girl Jimmy'd been dancing with? Jimmy heard scurrying above, as if rats were dancing in the rafters. Daring to stick his head outside the struts, he saw four tiny masks peering over a large beam in the ceiling. When his foot found its way under his new partner's and he stumbled into the ladder, all four tiny masks bobbed merrily.

Pulling his head inside the ladder's brace, Jimmy tried to take control of the dance, and did. But it was too late, since the ladder hovered over them and now had three braces extending between its two legs. They'd have to limbo to get out, and the tempo wasn't right for that. So they were trapped. Jimmy thought of kicking the ladder over even as one of the mustachioed men climbed it, then his penis ached, then he thought of running to the fan and unzipping. It wouldn't be as bloody as what the boy intended to do, after all. His partner had crooked her neck to watch the man climb. The guy carried a bulb the size of a cantaloupe, to replace one that had burned out. Good. The warehouse sorely needed illumination. Jimmy thought of a saint, say Aquinas, holding his hand in the familiar papal gesture, spreading a glow over the dance floor.

Mocking laughter emerged again, but when Jimmy managed to shift, all he saw was the old man lifting up the record player's needle to change records. Now Jimmy could even make out the old guy's sad, frog eyes. Was he on some type of moveable platform, to have gotten this close? Jimmy, that is. Or maybe the old geezer, that is. Relativity, that is. Light arrives before sound, so Jimmy knew right away that the old Hebrew had popped on some boogie-woogie, for his hair was flopping like the moons around Jupiter. But there was no getting that rhythm into the heads of any of the dancers: they all kept up their same pace, as if "Red River Valley" had never stopped. Maybe it was eight to the bar somewhere, but in this warehouse, it was one-two, one-two.

Odd, but both the boy and the huge fan had moved too. It would be easier for Jimmy to believe that he and his partner had shuffled back across the floor, except for the ladder still surrounding them. Light blasted on overhead, and the workman descended, farting on the sixth step, near Jimmy's left ear. It was greasy; he must have eaten onion rings at the drive-in for lunch. Is this what adulthood holds for me? Greasy lunches, tedious work-nights screwing in light bulbs? Oh, for the blessed relief of pre-dawn sleep and dreams, then. Jimmy tried to pick up the pace to escape the rancid odor, but for some reason his partner resisted. And new couples had gathered, since the light bulb was back on. They'd even beaten the moths back into the circle of light, maybe to peck their fingernails or their masks against the ladder's wood.

It was the boy, though, who really caught Jimmy's attention. Now he was Buddha-squatting directly in front of the fan, his hair lifted and thrown backwards. It even seemed that he was forced into a tilt by the strength of the wind. He, too, was picking up the boogie-woogie beat, for his shoulders and that of the old white-haired Jew bounced in syncopation.

One-two, one-two went everyone else.

"Listen! Stop and listen!" Jimmy yelled.

But no one did.

Then he realized that he hadn't yelled. Had he thought, maybe? The ladder evaporated—had some jealous couple stole it and placed it under another light bulb? Now the weirdest thing: the hick music was gone, and so was the boogie-woogie. The old Jew had placed the needle of a record by Wagner, "The Flying Dutchman." How was anyone supposed to dance to that? Don't Jews hate Wagner? Didn't Wagner hate Jews? Aquinas, he was before Wagner, after the Jews. It all twisted around fiendishly.

Jimmy discovered that it didn't make any difference—what was playing, that is—for his partner had deserted him. He nervously shifted his crotch: surely he didn't still have an erection. No, it was gone. Wait, he thought: I'm too young for erections. He glanced to the old man, who was swaying serenely to some *Flying Dutchman* movement. The old man grinned at him, though that was impossible, for the space between them had grown distant again. So he must be smiling at the Buddha boy, who was standing now, swaying also, staring into the fan, moving closer to its open face with each sway.

"No!" Jimmy shouted.

But no one listened. Instead, another girl tapped him on the shoulder. Was it the first one, the one with the frozen grin? If so, something had unfroze her grin and twisted it into a sardonic grimace. *Sardonic*, Jimmy thought. What's that? It was what the mask on the girl looked like, that's what it was. As they clasped to dance their one-two, her breath eased from jagged holes in her mask, smelling dankly of lichen and red-capped mushrooms. From the record player, the brass was crescendoing, the violins terwilliping. If possible, this "Flying Dutchman" crap seemed smarmier than "The Red River Valley."

"It's the sea," the girl said dreamily. Jimmy couldn't make out her eyes because of her mask. "It's the sea, and we're all floating in the waves, up and down, tossed and lost, like the stars overhead, crisscrossed."

One-two, one-two, buckle my shoe.

"What's my mask look like?" he asked, tilting it at her.

She appeared not to hear. It was as if she'd planted both ears in conch shells to immerse herself in the sea. One-two, one-two, and through and through her vorpal head went snicker-snack. One-two, one-two—though Jimmy was pretty sure this was waltz time again. The old Jew had abandoned the record player and now stood by the fan, resting his right hand on it as if he'd discovered the Ark of the Covenant. His head swept along with the insipid notes, rather like a bobbing, religious rubber ducky. The boy kept edging toward him and the fan.

"No!" Jimmy shouted again. Or he pretended to. Or he did and no one heard him. Moths kept pinging at the bare light bulbs. Jimmy saw the one closest to the door—he and his partner had drifted away—give off a blue flash. He supposed that the moths were shorting the bulbs out; that's why the two moustaches had to keep replacing them. Even now, they'd set up their ladder in another spot.

The girl with the sardonic smile had moved Jimmy and herself closer to the fan, elbowing through people. Jimmy recognized the girl who'd thrown the shoulder punch, and he stiffened. But she was with a completely different boy now. He recognized his baby-sitter, though she pretended not to see him. She was starry-eyed, just as if she were on the open sea with a roving sailor. He decided to try again.

"Your mask is pretty. My mask, what's it look like?"

"Words no good," the girl replied.

There was a great tangling screak. Warm liquid spattered Jimmy's face. Where had his mask gone? And the girl's hair was all bloody, with a bit of white and pink flesh caught in a brown curl. One-two. An arm landed between them, a slather of bowel to their left. One-two. A hand to their right, a head dropped hollowly to their rear. Jimmy turned, though the girl kept dancing without him. He stepped toward the head; it was the boy, and he too had been shorn of his mask. Jimmy nudged the head with his shoe, accidentally, he hoped, though there was no being certain that he hadn't kicked out from frustration. The boy's mouth was moving in motor reflex. Or was it gasping for breath? Or was it asking a question? Or giving an answer? Jimmy stooped and placed his ear next to the mouth until he felt wet heat ascend. There was a sound. Burbling? No, it was words. Jimmy pressed closer, feeling a bubble of blood or spittle burst against his earlobe. What language was it? German? French? Russian? Yiddish?

One-two.

The girl, she was standing straddle-legged and tugging at him. In her hand, she held his mask. She bent and he could feel her pressing it against his cheek.

One-two. Things always return.

She tried to slip the mask over his head. "Don't listen!" She yelled. "Don't! Hit's none of hit's true!"

Hit's? How long had it been since he'd heard someone say *"hit's"* for *"it's"*? Thirty years, since he'd left Kentucky. Thirty years. So he was fifty-four. Dazed, he let the woman pull him up and slip the mask back onto his head. They turned from the boy's still-working mouth to resume their dance. Hank Williams: "I'm so Lonesome I Could Cry." From overhead came rustling, maybe laughter. A scrap of paper floated down, landing with dark, enticing runes, half-covered, half revealed. But the sardonic girl was right: there wasn't a bit of it true. He didn't bother to pick the paper up, didn't bother glancing at the decapitated head, didn't bother to look toward the rafters. Not a bit of hit was true.

Coriolus

The Leavitt Brothers were normal enough pre-World War II public relations saps, except for one thing: their ability to delve—at least partly—into a person's future just from a handshake. It was this ability, on the second day of prepping some coastal city for the coming circus, that made the two warily consult one another during a breakfast of coffee, fried eggs, grits, jam and sausage-gravy over buttermilk biscuits (for they were in a Deep South town):

"Twenty-six, all of them without a timeline beyond a week."

"Twenty-eight for me. One of mine, he did have a long timeline, though. Twenty-eight out of twenty-nine."

The older brother, who'd spoken first, poured more sugar in his coffee, then more cream, then leaned forward to ask as the overhead fan whopped, since it was already hot at nine o'clock, "And that one was . . ."

"Worked for the railroad. Leaving town tomorrow."

The older brother, Ben, now sat back into the booth's wood until it creaked. "Well, we'll be leaving the day after the circus starts."

A whistle of a sigh escaped both their lips.

The circus would be setting up Thursday morning, opening Friday at noon. This was their routine: travel ahead, buy any licenses needed, arrange last minute advertising, secure local food vendors, and make the necessary bribes. The circus's overseer had found out the hard way that most folks over twenty-one didn't care for carny/circus types, so he'd hired the brothers in Lexington,

Kentucky, three years before. The brothers really didn't care for carny/circus types either, but the money was good and the travel was exciting for two hill boys originally from eastern Kentucky facing a life of coal-mining. They'd both done one summer in the mines. That was when and where they learned about their ability to tell the future, two days before shoring gave way, trapping forty-seven.

A waitress walked up and poured their coffee. She rubbed her hip against the older brother, Ben, who was a womanizer and had slept with her the night before. The younger brother Thomas—labeled Doubting Thomas by the overseer and the other circus folk—had heard her moaning until two in the morning through the cheap hotel room wall. Even through the walls her moans sounded fake. No doubt she was more interested in leaving this Hicksville city to go on the road with his brother Ben than in what was going on in bed. Unfortunately, that might happen, for Thomas had lied to his brother: there'd been two long lifelines of the thirty—not twenty-nine—that he shook, and hers was the other besides the railroad man's. Thomas, of course, didn't mention this to his brother, partly because he'd been surprised that she'd shaken hands with him at all—aggressive and masculine, especially for the South.

Both of them had three more people to see on this Monday; then they would report back to the circus overseer after driving through all afternoon to reach him. Emitting genetically identical belches from the jam, biscuits, and sausage gravy, the brothers stood up and left the greasy spoon to meet their last appointments.

Upon returning to their car at noon, Thomas couldn't believe his doubting nose, for he found the waitress, whose name was Loti Thompson, sitting in the back seat with a single maroon suitcase propping up her skinny elbows. Oh well. As the three of them drove out of town, her perfume swelled his sinuses, even with the windows open. On the two-lane, Ben kept reaching back to touch her leg until Thomas said he had to piss, please stop the car. He got out, walked behind a deserted farmhouse where a rattlesnake rattled then slunk off, and he took a piss. Returning to the car, he insisted on driving the remainder of the trip—for he feared that despite the waitress's long lifeline he'd gotten the futures wrong and Ben would wreck on the way to the circus from paying so much attention to her leg or ankle or whatever body part she was jiggling. Besides, Thomas liked driving through the Louisiana swamps, which lay on their way to outside Baton Rouge, to meet with the circus. Baton Rouge had come after New Orleans, where with the new city council they'd had to pay out more ready money than in any town the brothers had experienced in their three years with the circus. The Baton Rouge people must have gotten wind, because they weren't so cheap either. But the tannic water of the swamps drove all that money worry from Thomas's mind, and he practiced concentric-breathing. He'd found a book on yoga on his bed the last time he'd spent the night with the circus. He suspected Carlotta, the gypsy, had left it there.

Carlotta was standing outside the overseer's elaborately painted trailer when the two brothers met him on the makeshift redwood porch that he insisted on setting up directly upon each arrival the circus made, no matter how temporary the stay. As they shook hands with him, they exhaled in relief that his palm did not reveal the ice of imminent death. Carlotta had moved herself into Thomas's view, and judging from her faint smile she seemed to understand his reaction to the handshake. This unnerved the younger brother because Carlotta labeled herself a gypsy, although her skin was as fair and her eyes as blue as any mid-summer sky. Her raven hair was her ticket. Carlotta always unnerved Thomas, for her blue eyes inevitably captured both his esophagus and heart at their least glance. So he stared at her, some fifteen feet away, and watched her bend to pet her black male cat, her other ticket to gypsydom. His brother Ben elbowed him, and the overseer chuckled. Carlotta gave Thomas a grin as Ben tugged him inside the overseer's trailer so they could give their report.

"I don't understand why you don't go ahead and cork her," the overseer said. He was a large man, nearly three hundred pounds, with dark brown slicked-down hair. He owned the circus, though he used the title of overseer to throw people off in case of legal troubles. It was Carlotta who'd told Thomas several months ago that the overseer was really the owner.

"He's going to have to get him something to cork soon," Ben said. "I picked up a filly back in that town. Left her in the trailer we use. She's cleaning it up right now."

The overseer's brows gathered. "Bad luck to travel two men, one woman. You should let me hire her on, let her travel with Carlotta. What can this filly do? If she's pretty enough and doesn't have too bad a damned cracker twang, she can work tickets, if nothing else."

When they stepped out from the overseer's trailer nearly an hour later, Carlotta was still standing in the same position, holding her cat in her arms, his blackness nearly lost between the sunset and the dark maroon and purple swirls of her half-dress, half robe. In the distance, a tent dropped with a whoosh, followed by an odd cracking of timber. The overseer shook his head and strode angrily toward the sound. When the brothers stepped off the porch, Carlotta confronted Thomas, speaking loudly over the din of the circus being torn down and packed.

"Come have supper with me at my trailer."

Thomas nodded, barely hearing his brother's chuckle.

The outside of Carlotta's trailer was gaudily painted, like the overseer's, except hers insistently used shooting stars and moons and at least three Saturns. Its inside was lined with books and candles, and it always smelled vaguely of incense, since she held her readings in its main room. She and Thomas sat at a round marble tabletop that three polished red granite elephants held up. The thick top was cold, no matter the summer weather. An opened bottle of burgundy sat on it, between two glasses that looked purple and fractured, as if they were centuries old.

"Pour us wine," Carlotta said, pushing aside a heavy tapestry that revealed a tiny kitchen. A sweet smell of cooked honey filled the air, though the astringent punch of hot peppers whisped underneath. As Thomas poured the wine, Carlotta luxuriously twisted her hips and ladled lunch into a tureen shaped like a cupped hand wearing a huge, gaudy ruby ring. She set the tureen on the table with the ruby facing Thomas. Then she placed two beet-red plates and two shiny silver sets of utensils, being careful that the utensils were parallel. Thomas leaned toward the tureen, but Carlotta's red nails clutched at his wrist.

"Wine first," she said.

So they drank, Carlotta's eyes on Thomas the entire time. He finally told her about all the hands they'd shaken and their short lifelines. She bit her wine glass and nodded. He'd already told her about his and his brother's ability the same night she'd told him about the overseer being the owner. When they finished the first glass, she stood and closed the thick curtain to the kitchen. On the curtain—more of a Turkish rug, really—a lamb in an improbably blue and green field bleated open-mouthed and pitiful. Carlotta rubbed her cheek against the lamb; then she walked to pour more wine. In the small trailer, Thomas could feel heat from her hip flushing his cheek, so he set the wine down without drinking, after picking it up. She ladled out a dark goulash. At first it tasted heavy, as of blood. Thomas thought it must be the strange paprika. Then it tasted hot, as of peppers—enough to make his forehead break into a slight sweat, despite two fans. And then it was night, and he lay in her arms for the first time.

She hummed as he made love to her—not continually, but intermittently when he thought he was in his best stride. Thick, warm, salty water rose about his loins and then about his chin as she pulled him down atop her. The water ebbed and waxed, warmly lapping against his shoulder blades and back as if the real moon were toying with them, turning them willy-nilly into tidal pools. She stopped humming and cicadas chirped, and what he supposed was a bull alligator bellowed.

"You need me," she said.

Again she hummed as he made love to her, but this time she

inserted a word or phrase that seemed to purr from her mouth in a foreign lisp. And this time she crawled atop him. At one point, he looked up with a start, thinking her face was the full moon. *Gibbous* was a word that came to him from some magazine article, and he said it aloud. "Schatsie, schatsie, schatsie," she cooed melodically in response. He munched on her soft stomach, and soon tasted a rank mix of goat cheese and honey as her small pouch glowed luminescent over his head. When she stiffened, his body sank into cool moonsand, which oozed through his toes and out the small craters of his skin.

"You need me," she repeated, scooting along his chest and stomach.

And then she was silent as they made love, though her body writhed and coiled in alternating heat and cold, wet and dry, to the rhythm of the nearest oscillating fan. She nibbled his shoulder, his chest hair, his cheeks, his neck, his forearms, his hips, and his scrotum with such tiny bites that her incisors felt more like electric probes than teeth. A jolt hit them both, straightening them to their very toes, which curled back and scraped the other's ankle.

"We need one another," she said.

Tuesday morning, Carlotta went to find Loti and Ben. She brought Loti back and chased Thomas out, telling him to go help pull tents or drink with his brother, whichever. When he came back mid-afternoon, she chased him off again. And when he and Ben came back near sunset, Loti answered the trailer's door, swiveling her hips in a gypsy skirt. All in all, she was a more convincing gypsy than Carlotta, as long as she didn't string more than five words into a sentence that let her hick Southern accent betray her.

"Thomas, I'm going back with you. Ben, you and Loti are staying here to drive this trailer."

This was close enough to how they usually did things anyway, so Thomas and Ben agreed. Thomas could hear his brother wheezing in anticipation beside him: it was like Loti had changed into a new woman and he was getting a chance to cheat on her before he cheated on her. Thomas only hoped that Ben wouldn't wreck the trailer from gawking at Loti's makeover. Then he wondered if maybe he should let Carlotta drive their car for the very same reason: that he might crash from peeping at Carlotta's knees or her mysteriously small hands.

Thomas and Carlotta left in early pre-dawn on Wednesday so they would arrive in the town by mid-morning, to finalize a couple of arrangements. During the drive, Thomas found himself acting every bit as foolishly with Carlotta as his brother had with Loti, even more so, for Carlotta's dark hair puddled along with the middle of night in his lap as she took his penis into her mouth. His eyes twisted as he climaxed, barely keeping the headlights and the edges of the highway straight. When he touched Carlotta's hand a minute later, his eyes widened and his mouth dropped. How could he have missed—

"There were a sister and brother," Carlotta said, turning in his lap, cheek against his cock, almost speaking to it. "A forbidden love lay between them ever since they stumbled into puberty."

"They tried to fight it," Thomas said, "by running through fields together."

"Yes," Carlotta answered, "But the sister tripped over a root one day and the brother cradled her in his lap. They could no longer resist—"

"The Devil held them in his power."

"There is no Devil; only the cessation of dreams."

Cessation, Thomas thought, licking his tongue as if tasting the odd word. "That and death," he said, thinking of Carlotta's hand. He idly wondered what might happen if he shook his own hand. . . .

"Well yes, surely. Cessation, surely." Thomas had touched his own right hand with his left, then his left with his right. What he feared might happen, had. "But the brother and sister . . ." He licked his lips. "They only knew one another's body and the wind and the sun and the cooling rain. Cessation was unimportant to them."

"But their father the king sent them on an errand."

"Yes," Thomas agreed. "But they knew—"

"They knew—"

"Cessation." Thomas thought he spotted a deer alongside the road, but the car was past the spot already, so he stared at the huge yellow moon. "So instead of doing the king their father's errand they traveled . . ." He thought of the yellow moon and leaning back and lifting the car upwards so that it would shoot in that direction.

"They traveled to the Great Wall of China."

"Yes, and as they walked along that wall, for the first fifty miles he stared at her toes, for he loved them."

"Did he?" Carlotta asked.

Peripherally, Thomas thought he saw her placing her toes into the open passenger window to catch the night air; he for sure felt her squirming in his lap.

"Yes. And for the next fifty miles he bent to brush her calf, for he loved its tight, soft skin."

"Did he?"

For an answer, Thomas leaned and rubbed Carlotta's right calf, and the front wheel lurched into gravel. He and Carlotta laughed as he brought the car back to the road.

"And for the next fifty miles?"

"Her thigh. And then her hips, for there a secret bone on her pelvis protruded like a hill, and he loved to let his fingers climb that hill."

"Did he?"

For answer, Thomas rubbed his fingers over Carlotta's pelvis, bringing forth her sighs.

"What sort of night was it?" she asked. "Was it a night like this, sitting on the edge of morning?"

"Exactly like this. And the moon followed them like a faithful coon hound."

Carlotta chortled. "Like a *what?*"

Thomas explained hunting coons with a pack of hounds. He had gone with his two uncles after his father was killed by mustard gas during World War I. He explained the low musical howls when the hounds caught a scent, the sharp yelps as they closed, the coon's razor teeth, the torn flesh, the silvery glints of frenzy, the whimpers of the wounded hounds after the coon was killed.

"Did you eat the animal?"

"There was nothing left. And coons are greasy."

"Then what's the point?"

Thomas rested his hand on Carlotta's pelvis. "Exactly," he said.

They watched the moon following them for the next few miles until they entered a long curve and the moon then lay before them. Carlotta let out an unexpected howl. "Where are they now?" she asked.

"Who?"

"The brother and sister. Are they still walking the Great Wall? What part of her body is he loving? Her lips? Her eyes? Her—"

"Can you drive?"

So they changed places, and Thomas's head lay in Carlotta's lap, his hands tugging at her panties. He stopped suddenly. "Did you shake hands with my brother?" Thomas couldn't make out whether Carlotta nodded yes or shook her head, so he asked again.

"No. Did you?" Carlotta let up on the gas.

"No." Thomas could smell Carlotta's sex and her moisture. She had used perfume that smelled like the incense in her trailer. He gave a quick lick to her thigh, then a kiss. "It's better that way, that he doesn't know, I mean."

"But we know."

"We have each other."

They both thought of the waitress, Loti Thompson.

"They have left the Great Wall," Thomas said. "Now they're climbing in the Hanging Gardens of Babylon. He is carrying her. He is licking every inch of her body, and kissing, and blowing hot, then cold air onto it."

"She tells him what they are passing. There are ferns that droop like slender Australian pines. They catch in a breeze and make a sweeping sound on the marble floors."

"Weeping? Marble?"

"Sweeping. But marble, yes, of course. It is cool. She has sat on the hanging garden's floor and opened herself to him." As if in demonstration, Carlotta shifted her right foot off the accelerator and pushed steadily with her left, widening her legs. She inhaled quickly as Thomas nibbled the tiniest bit of flesh off her thigh. "And there are animals. . . ."

"Coons?"

She laughed gutturally and lifted her middle against his mouth, while gripping the steering wheel. "Cats. Black cats, white cats, gray cats." She laughed again. "And snakes, of course."

"Snakes?"

"The Egyptians kept pet snakes to fend off rats from their grain, why wouldn't the Babylonians? Snakes are so lovely and long."

Soon, Carlotta's breathing quickened and she let off the gas, coasting to the side of the road. They stopped under a canopy of live oaks, where crickets were scratching and distant bullfrogs croaking, though it might have been alligators, since they were far enough south. With her four sharp yells, the canopy became quiet.

"Now they are in the Temple of Diana. Demetrius, a silversmith, is cursing the Apostle Paul, who wants to tear down the temple." Carlotta tugged Thomas's ear and he sat up.

"He *should* be cursed then."

They kissed soft, then hard, then soft.

"That is the first time I've ever tasted myself," Carlotta said.

The crickets had started back up, and the two of them were surprised to find that the car had stalled out. Carlotta crawled over Thomas so he could restart the motor, for he explained that it was temperamental. And it was: he had to push the starter button four times before the engine caught, and he'd jiggled the gas pedal as if he were correcting his breathing.

"Where are they now?" he asked as he pulled back onto the highway.

"They are in a small boat, rowing, sailing toward the Colossus of Rhodes."

"Sailing? I thought they were rowing."

"Sailing, rowing, floating. Their goal is the same."

"To become one with the coon?"

"To become one."

"Yoga? Buddha?"

"If you want. Love."

"If you want."

A figure in white appeared on the highway, making them both catch their breaths. The figure was quite small, and partly bounced as it walked.

"It's a boy," Carlotta said, almost relieved, for she feared they had conjured a ghost.

They pulled to the side of the road and the boy stared at them, like a deer caught in their headlights.

"It's all right, son," Carlotta called through the open window. "Do you need help?"

"My father," he said. He pointed up the road.

"He's hurt?"

The boy nodded and they coaxed him into the car. His head glowed silver-white under the full moon.

"My sister's with him. Our mother left us. Daddy wrecked the car."

On impulse, Thomas reached for the boy's hand. Upon touching it he smiled broadly.

"Yes," Carlotta agreed, after looking into the boy's moonlit eyes.

Not more than a minute later they came upon the car, an old roadster with an open rumble seat. It slanted into a small ditch. The father was pacing in the road, with his daughter tugging his hand. In the mixture of moonlight and headlamps, the two looked to be caked with flour. The man raised a pint of whiskey and the girl said something. Carlotta and Thomas heard the man reply, "Just one more, that's all. Just one more, so's I can forget her. You understand, don't you?"

The boy jumped out of the car and ran toward his father. "I told you I'd find help. I told you."

His father held the pint midway to his mouth and looked from the boy to Thomas and Carlotta. He lowered the pint.

"Did you come from the tavern? Did she send you? I told her I'd leave her damned daddy's damned roadster at the house. I'm taking the truck and the kids to Tennessee. . . ." He turned to look at the car. "I ought to burn the damned thing, though." He heaved the whiskey bottle at the car. Oddly, the pint bottle didn't break, for it hit a tire.

"Daddy!" The boy and the girl each had a hand they were tugging on.

"I'll make some coffee," Carlotta said. The brothers always carried a pot since they were persnickety about their coffee and greasy spoon brew didn't always agree with them. She got out and called to the children. "Do you want to help me find some wood for a fire? We're going to brew your father some coffee."

"Will the car run? If we get it out of the ditch, I mean," Thomas asked, heading toward the man as Carlotta and the two children walked into the woods.

"So you're not from the tavern? She didn't send you?"

"We're with the circus that's coming day after tomorrow. We're heading into town to make final arrangements."

"Circus," the man said. He started for the bottle, but stopped. "Did she say she could make some coffee out here?"

"She did."

"Well, I suppose the car'll run. Sure, if we can get it out. The boy and me tried, but . . ."

"If he can drive, he can give it some gas while we push."

Ahead, they heard Carlotta and the girl laughing.

"He can drive, all right. He's almost a man." The man stooped and then lifted to shout, "Ain't you, son?"

Thomas stood near the man now, and as the man again bent for the pint, Thomas said, "Why don't you let me take that? You've got the boy and the girl and a lot of driving if you're going to make it to Tennessee." When Thomas took the pint from the man, he brushed his hand. The sign wasn't there. So he would live. The moon seemed to wink at Thomas. "That's what you're going to do, isn't it? Drive the children to Tennessee?"

The man looked at the pint in Thomas's hand and nodded.

"Good. Let's get the car out of that ditch."

By the time they pushed the car out and ascertained that it had suffered nothing more than a broken headlamp, Carlotta and the girl had finished the coffee.

"She did it by herself. Said she knew just how you liked it," Carlotta observed, placing her hand on the girl's golden curls.

"She's straight out of a fairy tale," the man said. Then he looked at Carlotta and Thomas. "And I guess you two are too, what with your circus and coming here in the nick of time, saving me from getting pie-eyed goose-liver drunk and the kids from having to see that. I'm obliged." He glanced to his children, and they each said, "Thank you."

The man assured Carlotta and Thomas that his house wasn't but a mile away and that he and the children would be off within an hour, thanks to the coffee. Carlotta and Thomas followed them until they turned onto a dirt road. The girl stood up in the rumble seat and waved at them. Thomas tooted the horn.

"I gave the little girl forty dollars," Carlotta said. "All I had. She said their mother had stolen most of their money to spend on some man."

"I have enough of the circus's money for our last night. . . . The moon, it's so beautiful shining on the road." He honked the horn again, in a shave-and-a-haircut rhythm to celebrate the moon. "Where are they now?" he asked as Carlotta scooted toward him.

"They've passed the Lighthouse on the Isle of Pharos, where

they saved three sailors. The wind is at their backs, and they can see the Colossus of Rhodes, its muscular legs and its calm, all-seeing eyes. It smiles, you know. It smiles in the oddest of ways."

"Not a smirk?"

"No, not that. It's not laughing, either. It's just smiling out at the waves and at the ships and at the gulls and seabirds."

"Porpoises?"

"Yes, there is a school of them jumping."

Carlotta licked Thomas's arm where he'd cut himself pushing the car. To him, it sounded as if she were purring. In the east, a layer of gray painted itself over the black. To their right, night lay curling on itself.

Though he could smell coffee in Carlotta's hair, he thought she was asleep. He drank the dregs from his cup, tasting the bitter grit of the grounds and smiling to himself, remembering that the girl had brewed it. . . .

"They're nearing The Valley of Kings in Egypt. The Valley of Death and all its pyramids."

Carlotta's voice startled Thomas, who was nearly asleep and about to drive off the road. He jerked the steering wheel back. "They were just in the Greek islands. They didn't see the Parthenon?"

"Oh yes, they saw it. And they laughed at all its wisdom."

"And Rome. The Great Colosseum?"

"Those too. And they laughed at the gladiators and the Christians and the lions. But now they are staring at the pyramids, those tombs. Do you want me to drive?"

Thomas nodded and sighed at the same time. So they pulled over, and Carlotta drove them onward as the sun came up, its eye fiery like that of the lamb on Carlotta's thick curtain. Why was the lamb's eye so fiery, its mouth so pitiful and bleating?

Soon they were in town. They passed a post office, and Carlotta suggested that they turn around, for she wanted to send her two sisters each a post card. Thomas agreed that he too, should send his brother one. Inside the cigar-smelling office they showed each other what they'd written:

Carlotta's cards both read: *For two days, the sun and wind have been at my back, the moon has lain before me, and I have found love. What more could I ask?*

And Thomas's read: *Carlotta and I have seen the nine wonders of the world. Yes, there are nine. I hope you will see as many.*

They checked into Hotel Drake. Or was it Drake Hotel? They knew there was no sense in finalizing the circus's business, for when Thomas brushed the clerk's hand, no future lay in it, howsoever the hotel's name was oriented, backwards or forwards. Still, they went out into the town and finished their jobs. After lunch, the two of them walked up the hotel's red-carpeted stairs, opened their second floor window and rested in one another's arms to make love until their time came.

"The moon is hidden behind clouds tonight," Carlotta observed as night finaly came.

"We can't tell whether the man in it is smiling or frowning."

"That's right. We can't tell whether the woman in it is smiling or frowning."

"Like the Sphinx and the Colossus."

"Their last Wonder, the tenth."

"Ah, not nine then."

Less than two hundred miles off the coast, a force-four hurricane was building. Just before dawn and at high tide, it would make landfall and move slightly north, then stall over the town, pulling water from a huge lake backward over overturned cars, boats, rubble, corpses, and already standing ocean water, water that had plenty of places to go, but no ability to leave.

The Soft Queen
of Dissolution

Robert DuFresne is sitting on a stool in a half-Mexican bar, studying its eclectic walls. Everything hanging there, he's been told, has a story. The broken blue police flashers, for instance, tell a story that Robert is intimately familiar with. Three years ago when he first came to this town he got drunk in a bar down the street and was riding his motorcycle back to a hotel when a cop tried to pull him over. Robert made a sharp and lucky turn down an alley, the cop drove into a ditch across from this bar and hit a phone pole, knocking off his flashers and totaling the car by bending its frame.

There's more to the story, too, because the cop was the brother-in-law of the girl that Robert's now dating, and though she got divorced two years back the cop still looks out for her. Robert squeezes lime into his beer and drinks it, wondering when she'll show.

The cop ex-brother-in-law always looks at Robert askance, which leaves Robert in a state of eternal vigilance, waiting for the other shoe to fall when the cop recognizes that he's the one who made him wreck one of the town's seven police cars. Robert sold his motorcycle directly after that night and walked to his new job at the architecture firm for eight months until he bought a car; he had enough from his savings and the sale of the motorcycle to pay for a used one without taking out a loan.

Robert smells perfume and thinks that it's Regina's, but it's not. In fact, he can't figure out who's wearing it, since the only two women in the bar are sitting catty-wampus from him, under the crucifix hung on the wall. When Robert first time sat in that booth nearly three years back, he thought the crucifix was blasphemous, maybe a joke in bad taste. But the owner's name is Jesús, and Hay-Zeus is a good Catholic who likes to keep his namesake watching over matters.

The cross is made of yellow pine, and the Jesus corpse is made of yellow plastic that looks like ivory. The corpse glows in the dark, maybe from isotopes gathered from the first atomic blast tested up the road. Big Boy, wasn't that the name of the test? Jesús always wonders why they didn't just go full steam ahead and drop Big Boy on the Japanese right away, noting that America only had two left. Fine, Robert answers: Hiroshima, Nagasaki, and Tokyo? Jesús always shrugs and says, "Fuck the Japs."

Jesus—not Hay-Zeus—has been on Robert's mind a lot lately. The cross is a story too, isn't it? Did Jesus really die for love? Robert is 33, just like Jesus. Robert's been coming to his apartment at night and thinking, 33. That's it, just envisioning the numbers side by side. Sometimes they dance in a wobbly twirl, but mostly they just stand side by side and sulk. He thinks that maybe he's getting suicidal or crazy.

There's a framed blueprint hanging on the wall across from where Robert's sitting. He can see it in the mirror. It's from the firm he works for, the Mateo Bros. Supposedly it's the blueprint from the first building the firm designed. Juan Mateo has befriended Robert and tells him that they used to draft blueprints by etching out the blue with a sharp pen knife instead of using a computer program like Robert uses now. Robert's never been sure whether Juan's having the young gringo from New Mexico State U on or not. The blueprint's got a story too. It was for a restaurant that opened in Santa Fe. The owner got involved with one of his waitresses and began socking money to her left and right. Trouble was, he had a pregnant wife and five children, being a good Catholic and this being before birth control at any rate. Trouble was, the money he was socking to this bombshell blonde waitress was coming out of the employees' social security co-pay that he was supposed to make as their boss. The IRS padlocked the Mateo Bros. designed restaurant one morning at sunrise. That evening, the owner was dead from a .38 he'd put in his mouth.

"Whatcha doin'?"

It's Regina, and Robert perks up at her 24 year-old lilt.

"Looking at stories on the wall."

"Stories?" She shifts her lithe boy-like frame before him.

"You know, the tales that things on the wall represent." He is about to point out the stuffed armadillo, the bar's favorite tale, but Regina scoots against him, rubbing her rear end into his crotch.

"How's that for a tail?" She leans into him and bats eyes that seem to grow bigger every time he sees her. Her perfume zaps him for sure now; he feels it in his toes.

"Best one in here," Robert assures her.

"In *here?*"

"In the town."

"The *town?*"

"In the whole state, including every coed at UNM."

Regina twists and drinks some of his beer. He puts his palm on her bare arm; its softness makes him feel like he busts rocks apart with a sledgehammer ten hours a day instead of working at a computer. He can feel himself getting hard as she shuffles her hips from thigh to thigh and pushes in. She grins on feeling the start of his erection and hops onto the stool next to him, waving three fingers at Hay-Zeus, who's talking with some old guy with white hair. Robert blinks at the shock of the guy's head. It too seems to glow with isotopes.

"Stories. Jesús'll put anything on these walls, as long as it has a story, no matter how lousy the ending," Regina says, oddly.

Jesús carries a Heineken to Regina. She's the only customer in the bar who drinks that European import, other than an occasional college kid who strays down on a joy-ride.

"Your ex came in here Saturday night," Jesús tells Regina.

She takes the beer, puts it to her forehead, then sips it. "Let me guess: he was drunk."

Jesús smiles, but it's not a happy smile. "I heard that Tomas threw him in jail after he left, for WUI."

"WUI?"

"Walking under the influence."

Robert and Regina laugh, and Robert thinks that their laughter is like a Tex-Mex country song.

"Are you serious?" she asks finally.

"As serious as leprosy on a armadillo."

Tomas is Regina's ex-brother-in-law, the cop who drove his patrol car into the ditch. The ditch has since been filled and some civic-minded person has coaxed a squadron of cactus to grow there. Tomas, Regina always claims, is the one who convinced her to divorce her husband. Supposedly, Tomas' wife and the rest of her family haven't had anything to do with the guy for the last two years.

Hay-Zeus is now behind them, carrying beers to the pair of women sitting under Jesus. One of the women licks her lips lewdly and runs her fingers along Jesus's skinny legs on the cross, but only after Hay-Zeus turns to wait on three customers who've just sat under the two-foot tall hornet's nest. Everyone knows better than to make fun of the crucifix when Hay-Zeus is watching.

That hornet's nest has to be a story, too, though Robert's never heard it. The nest must be from upstate, since it's too hot and dry here.

"South New Mexico calling Robert. Have you beamed the spaceship into Roswell yet, Commander?"

"Sorry, Regina. I was just wondering about the hornet's nest."

"That's easy. Jesús and his wife found it on their honeymoon. Two weeks later the Japanese bombed Pearl Harbor and Jesús joined the navy. When he came back, his wife had gone."

"Run off?"

"No one knows. When Jesús gets drunk he swears she was kidnapped by aliens, that she only left him the hornet's nest because it scared the aliens."

They spend the night at Regina's house. It's left from her divorce, since her husband didn't want it because it's so small. Maybe, Robert thinks, it scared him. The thing that Robert likes best about staying with Regina besides her boyish hard breasts is how he rests his palm on her protruding hip bone after they make love. When he puts his palm there this night, he gazes out the window and sees the moon and thinks of the old guy with the white hair at the end of the bar. Robert hears his bowels move and blushes, even in the dark. He imagines the old geezer laughing.

Three nights later they're at Jesús's bar again. It's a Thursday. For lunch, Robert's boss (the remaining Mateo brother) and two other workers had split half-a-dozen tins of sardines with jalapenos. Robert helped eat them as they sat behind the stucco building watching a storm brew up north while they sweated. Robert's felt woozy ever since.

In fact, his first beer and lime makes his stomach clench.

Regina started earlier in the day. He can see this the moment she walks into the bar, loose enough to bump the door. Something's on her mind. At seven o'clock, Tomas walks in, pats Regina on the shoulder and tells Robert what a lucky guy he is. "Your ex is still in jail, by the way, Regina. He's got himself in a fight while he's been in—twicet, as the cowboys say."

By nine o'clock, Robert wants to go home because his stomach's so sour. He's only had four beers. Regina's had maybe seven. He's lost count. By ten o'clock, since it's still a week until payday for most people in the town, the bar's emptying. This includes Tomas, who once more tells Robert what a lucky guy he is.

"If he's got the sense to realize it," is Regina's return comment. Tomas smiles. He's got a gold tooth that Robert's never noticed before. Robert wonders if the real tooth was knocked out the night he ran the police cruiser into the ditch.

"Watch this," Regina says half an hour later. She motions for

Jesús, giving her famous three-finger lilt. He bends into the cooler, but she shouts that she doesn't want another beer, that she's got something for him to put on the wall. Or maybe she said on the ceiling, Robert's not sure, since his head is hurting too now.

When Jesús walks down, she pulls her satiny blue bra off in one sweep, peeling it from under her red t-shirt without a ripple. Robert and Jesús both stare at it, her. She might as well have made the Statue of Liberty disappear. Robert feels a pain in the right wall of his stomach. He can't imagine how she slipped the bra off; it doesn't make geometrical sense. How did she get the shoulder straps off without undoing them?

"On the ceiling, by the fan," Regina says, dangling the blue bra. "And look." From her small purse, she pulls out a queen of hearts with some fishing line attached to it. She pins it to one cup of the bra. So she's planned this.

Jesús shakes his head. "Your mother'd be proud. But your daddy—"

"Oh, Jesús, you know that Daddy'd be jumping to reach it every night by the time the sun started down, even if the ceiling fan lopped off his hand. Or his head."

Jesús grins. It strikes Robert that Jesús too has a gold tooth that Robert's either missed for the past two years or has forgotten about. But then, Robert's not sure the gold glint wasn't a trick of the dim light and the dirty bar mirror.

"Whooooo-hooo!" a customer at the end of the bar shouts, finally noticing the bra, still spinning in Regina's right hand. It's not the guy with the white hair, he's just looking mildly on, like maybe there's something more interesting happening outside the front door or window.

"I'm not getting between you and your man," Jesús says, raising brown palms and refusing the bra that Regina tries to pass to him. "You want it up there, fine. Either you or him puts it up, not me."

So Regina climbs on Robert's shoulders like they're playing horse and nails her bra into the ceiling, once she's found a spot where the fan will twirl the playing card about. As she does this the handful of customers in the bar cheer. She bounces on Robert's shoulders, waving like a political candidate.

"No, now both of you leave," Jesús says with a smile just when they start to return to their barstools. "Go give that bra a story. Ride down to the river and make a baby. Dance in the streets and get arrested. Spend the night howling in the desert like coyotes. Don't go driving drunk and get killed, though. That's not the kind of story I mean."

"We'll have a story for you next week," Regina says. "One way or another."

Robert burps and tastes sardines and jalapeños.

So what happens next is:

"Marry me."

"Huh?" Robert says. They've just gotten out the bar's door and a white car across the street is starting up. For some reason the car reminds Robert of a Roman chariot.

Regina bumps Robert with her hip. "You heard me. Marry me. This is the new millennium, the Age of Aquarius. Women can say what they want, ask what they want."

"I . . . I gotta think, Gina."

"*Re*-gina. Fine. Think all you want at your apartment." She says something else, but he's telling her how much his stomach aches and his head hurts so he doesn't hear.

She's in her car and gone.

So that's the story. A For Sale sign on her house, a blonde realtor who won't tell Robert anything about the seller or where she went, a shrug from the brunette veterinarian where she worked, who adds that she wrote Regina a letter of recommendation for college, a letter that she'd take back now, since Regina quit without giving notice. "You want a job?" the vet will offer. When Robert shakes his head and asks what college, the veterinarian answers, "Any. Dear Registrar. To Whom It May Concern. Dear Pet Owner. That kind of letter."

So for three weeks Robert will stare at the satiny blue bra. He will tell Jesús about her proposal to him right outside that door, about the sardines and jalapeños and his stomach. Tomas will walk in and shrug. He won't have heard from her either.

Jesús will tell Robert the story about the hornet's nest. Regina had gotten it a bit wrong: his wife hadn't left it for him: she'd sold it for two dollars to a neighbor. She'd sold everything in their house. And tried to sell the house to boot. Jesús paid the neighbor three bucks and got it back. "The Hornet's nest," Jesús adds, "not the house, though I never really got it back even though it never left."

"Where'd you find it in the first place," Robert will ask. "The hornet's nest. Up in the Sangre de Cristos mountains?"

"Mountains?" Looking at the nest bulging outward from the wall behind Robert, Jesús will grunt a harsh laugh and make a motion of spitting. "No, on *la luna*. I thought it was the sign of good fortune and love and sweet kisses to come." Jesús slaps his rag on the bar. "It was the double big sign of shit."

Robert will offer Jesús three dollars for the satiny blue bra and the queen of hearts playing card. He imagines that the bra will still have Regina's perfume clinging to it. He imagines that the queen of hearts will bring him luck. Jesús will lean over the bar, his breath smelling of cloves and cigars. "You don't want neither one, amigo. Take the hornet's nest instead. Free. On the house, yes? Ha-ha. That will make for you a better story where to stop. Just take it and remember la luna and the double sign of shit. That's where it all stops."

A Masque for
the Fields of Time

It's a movie, see, 'cause all life's a movie, struttin' across the silver screen, full of sound and fury and pain. Some monkey wrote that at his typewriter a long time back. Like I said, it's a movie, so let me give you a panoramic shot, ok? I mean, you can live with that, right?

So let's start with this field at evening. There's going to be some nuns moving queen-sized air mattresses onto it soon in a goofball mystical charade, but for now, just see the field and its grass, scorched tan from the summer's heat, and already trampled—in an Einsteinian timewarp anticipation of the nuns, I guess. This already-trampled field, it's enclosed by imposing rows of large water oaks on two sides, a dirty granite building on a third, and you on the fourth. Place the granite building silver-screen right, the oaks silver-screen left and way, way back. This near side you're inspecting the field from is important, so dolly the camera back until a stone footbridge with two supporting arches comes into sight. See yourself leaning hunch-backed over the bridge's low stone wall? That quaint stone bridge leads into a portico between the granite building and a new building that's just appeared as the camera keeps backing—Whoa! That's enough retreating for now or things will become too real, like a damned maze.

The new building that appeared is constructed with dark

maroon bricks. Now, if you'll just forget the camera and about-face your hunched-over body and cross to the bridge's other side, you can resume your hunch and glance down to find that you and the bridge span a cobblestone square with four long rows of oaken tables and benches. The tables are skinny, as if purposefully constructed to warn diners against gluttony. To the right of the tables, level with you from your hunched perch on the bridge, is something of a natural cliff with discretely embedded boulders and scrub brush to baffle erosion. Atop this cliff runs a narrow street. No cars on it, though. Save them for later. Okay? To your left—now that you've about-faced—is that same portico the bridge leads to, plus the same two buildings, one granite, one dirty maroon brick. Gather your courage and un-hunch yourself to scramble up on the sturdy rock wall. Now do a half gainer, jumping to catch hold of the airborne camera still hovering above. By helicopter, does that make you happy? Now let it pull you away, flying backward over the square, away from the bridge and the field and the picnic tables. You'll soon see a large red-, blue-, and yellow-tiled house on the corner of two streets. The kind of old house that someone who made money from bootlegging in the 1920's might have built, or maybe someone who held stock with the railroads in the late 1800's. Something shadowy on the opposite side of the street obscures this mirthful house from anyone sitting on the picnic benches down in the cobblestone square. Well hell, of course! It's the maroon brick building, two or maybe three-stories. If not for those maroon bricks and three filmy windows I'd guess it to resemble the windowless, blank granite marvel where the Spanish Inquisition was held in Madrid. Not as tall, but as austere. Screw verisimilitude because, see, it's all become too real already. Like I warned you, life's a goddamned maze. And look, a declining cobblestone road runs by this maroon building, descending alongside the four rows of skinny picnic tables and heading under the bridge you were standing on. Who knows where this cobblestone road might lead? The field? Another town? It's vague like the other end of the bridge, the one away from the portico and two buildings. Let's keep it vague. *The simple life, the simple life, a daisy, two kids, and a wife.* Some monkey wrote that too, no doubt. Maybe on the same typewriter.

Come on, forget the lousy poetry and keep hovering in that dolly with the camera; hell, flap your arms like Icarus if that makes you feel secure, though I thought the helicopter would solve your qualms. The four-bladed ones are more unstable and are prone to internal stress fractures, did you know? No, don't look up to count! Don't. Keep staring below: there's just one more panorama we need, so pull on back. There, see? It's the shore of a large lake. Don't worry about how this fits. Remember that we're talking movie, right? The lake's just one more set. Its shoreline is important, though. We need that shoreline for a scene that's going to stir you spiritually, a scene that's going to inflame our semi-protagonist—of sorts—emotionally.

OK, got all that down now? A field, a bridge, two narrow streets on either side of four rows of picnic tables—one street going up, one street going down—a mirthful tile house, two austere buildings hodgepodged together, lots of cobblestone, and a lake. Ready? I hope so, 'cause we're jumping in, *in media res.* That means in the middle of things, which is where things always start if you think about it—unless we're talking Big Bang, and even that must have interrupted some one's or some thing's Big Sleep.

The Masque Cometh:

Scene 1:

Cut to a classroom. Just toss it inside the maroon brick building. Don't give it any windows that the kids can daydream out of though, 'cause with this being the opening scene, we want to keep everyone focused. Look! There's our semi-protagonist. She's wringing her hands and walking back and forth in front of twenty or so kids. She's a nun and she's young, with a high forehead, clear complexion, and falcon gray eyes—I told you this was a movie; but, hey, these types do exist. Listen, she's speaking to the class:

"Flannery O'Connor was a good Catholic. She died in 1925. That's almost a century ago."

"Sister! Sister!"

This hissing comes from a kid. Would you like to be in this movie/masque? You really should be, you know. Fine, be the kid. Hey, I have to warn you, sister (just in case that's your sexual choice), that this kid's male, so cross your legs and don't go peeing or menstruating and ruining the illusion. It's important that he's male; he can't be female or unisex. You'll see why.

"Sister! Sister!"

Sister Anne wrings her hands and looks for a window. Of course, there is none, and her falcon gray eyes skitter, wanting to soar, wanting to dive. She can see this squirming boy won't stop with his hissing, so she acknowledges him, trying to keep her eyes steady.

"What, Danny?"

"Tommy. Tommy Daniels, Sister." The boy licks his boy lips to whet his courage. "Sister, Flannery O'Connor died in 1964."

"Oh no, Daniel. Flannery O'Connor . . . she never could have lived through the Second World War. She was much too sensitive. It would have been too much for her."

Tommy, our student—you!—screws up his eyes, trying to follow the nun's logic. Then Tommy remembers that Flannery O'Connor wrote a story about people who were displaced by the Second World War. Precocious child, aren't you? But what's with this nun, having eleven-year olds reading some crank like Flannery O'Connor?

"Uh, sister, she wrote a story called 'The Displaced Person' that's about someone coming to America after that war."

In sudden fury, Sister Anne knocks a metal globe off her desk. It bounces twice on the unpolished wood floor then hits a young girl's knee, causing her to pucker and wince. "Get out!" Sister Anne points to Tommy, but her flickering eyes scan all the young males in the room.

"Now!" she shouts. "All of you!"

The girls misinterpret and start to leave alongside the boys. Sister Anne's too surprised to do more than aspirate an, "Not you girls, no, I'd never, I didn't . . ."

As Tommy passes her to run into the sunlight toward some distant playground, (You do hear a seesaw's creaking metal joints, don't you? And don't you feel that summery breeze?); as Tommy passes her, he sees that she's fumbling with the large crucifix attached to her waist, rubbing the face of Jesus with her thumb. Is she trying to suffocate our good Lord? Tommy—you!—wonders if this might be the case. He turns with concern.

"Sister, I'm sorry. You shouldn't get so upset about a stupid date, anyway. Time's just a small number squatting on a big long line. Descartes said that." This kid's pushing the pale with his wisdom, isn't he? More of a hermetic messenger than any real child. But then, have you ever stopped to look into their eyes? Children, I mean. Have you ever listened to the way the little brats always drone something portentous and unpleasant in their screams and laughter? They're all messengers, I'm telling you.

Trembling, Sister Anne lifts the crucifix like a dagger. Tommy runs off before she can jab his pupil. And believe you me, he doesn't stop to worry about any pun on that last word.

Do you mind if we re-take the entire scene's ending from another angle? And play the sound back too? You might be considering what Wagner or Berlioz we could play, too. But first, let's change the scene a bit so it doesn't become boring:

Re-take, Scene one:

A blackboard pushes against Sister Anne's back. She hits her head slowly against it, smelling each boy as he passes, repressing waves of nausea, thinking of, thinking of—exactly what she doesn't want to think of. A voice forces her eyes open. That same hissing Tommy-voice.

"Sisssssss, you shouldn't let a little date or apple upset you. Just numbers, just so many arithmetic examples in a field. Three apples plus two bananas plus three dates equal—"

We can stop there. Take note of what Tommy said and make sure that *you* don't let a little thing like a date upset *you*, because the set is going to undergo several spinning time shifts involving decades at least, centuries or eons at most—if we can afford the costuming changes.

Scene two:

Sister Anne jabs her crucifix into the doorjamb, and with horror realizes that she'd been trying for the young boy's right eye. What was his name? Danny? Timmy? And where is he now? She spots him pushing a whirl-around full of boys and girls in the distance, all of them screaming and laughing. Or is he on the baseball diamond, tossing a softball? Or is he . . .

" . . . Mother Superior, I'm requesting to be reassigned to the kitchen."

"Why, my child? You've only been teaching one week." This Mother Superior, a woman well into her seventies, can call just about anyone she wants "child," and our semi-protagonist is certainly no exception, being in her early twenties.

"Oh Mother Superior, I hate men! I hate men so much that I hate every boy in my classroom! I . . ." Sister Anne is at a loss for words, thinking how she almost jabbed one male in the eye.

Now, the following line should be intoned importantly:

"Let us not forget that Christ was a man, child."

Sister Anne feels the crucifix, its foot bent where she indeed did jab the doorjamb. She rubs her thumb heavily over Jesus' face, hoping to suffocate him or at least make him cry out, "Mother, Mother, why hast Thou forsaken me?"

Suddenly someone holds Sister Anne's elbow. It's the Mother Superior. She's leading Anne toward the field where the nuns are putting out air mattresses to sleep in the open, like St. Francis and St. Clare. This charade might be the very thing that gets Mother Superior retired at last, many of the nuns hope. But for now, she's concerned with her twenty-year-old ward. "Teaching boys is your cross, Sister Anne. You must bear it for the love of Christ. Now, go help the other sisters."

Scene Three:

A shift comes now. Drop the sun a degree or so, if you want. Some students are climbing the stone steps of the bridge you were on moments before. The boys are from Mineola Catholic Boy's High and they've come—God knows why—to serenade the nuns. One boy, whose acne pits render his skin an alligator poacher's prize, says to a teacher, "Fadda, dis is one time youse ain't gonna tell me to keep quiet, is yaz?" This boy went through seventeen years of speech coaching for that lousy Bronx accent, so you better believe in it. But just wait until you hear him sing—like sugar water.

The priest, who may not even be a priest but simply a brother of a teaching order, or maybe not even that, but simply a salaried layperson who can't find a better job, playfully cuffs the boy's shoulder, being careful to avoid his acne, which—well, is it contagious? The other students all line up on the bridge and face the skinny empty oaken benches where the nuns will be eating their supper. Why don't you drop down and stand there with the students? Well, yeah, they are jumpy like toads. They're teenage boys, after all. I don't blame you for not wanting to associate too intimately. So do another half-gainer and just float out again to grab the camera and hover. Forget the four-bladed helicopter. (I'm sorry; I didn't want you to notice.) Forget it because you're getting into this Icarus bit, aren't you? Pace yourself, be careful, keep self-praise at a low roar. Remember how Icarus didn't have too happy an end, internal stress and metal fatigue doesn't confine itself to machinery, you know.

By now, traffic is starting to ascend the street directly to screen left, the street that ascends beside the cobblestone square where the nuns nightly and publicly eat in what the Mother Superior considers a work of Christian evangelism. Sometimes they even eat outside in light rain, as a type of public penance. *Retirement, retirement,* the nuns and novices mumble every night before breaking bread in the open air.

To return to the boys: Lord knows that they better have strong voices, because two cabbies on the ascending street are honking their horns and squealing their tires in a great show of impatience to impress their fares. And there's a young couple pumping one of those double-seat bicycles, wobbling precariously near the street's edge as they pass both cabs and a line of cars. A stone pops under their front tire and they nearly tumble. Look out!

Scene Four:

Down where this street starts its ascent, two motorcyclists have dismounted, their backs to the square where the nuns will be eating. Their bikes, still running, occasionally burp. The two motorcyclists wear blue sunglasses, even though the sun is pushing into evening. A young girl of Japanese heritage approaches and dons sunglasses of immense darkness, each blackened shade in the shape of an equilateral triangle. In contrast to the sunglasses, her small body is ruled by her hips, her breasts, and her fluidity.

"Look at this getup," she chirps to the two brutes standing by their motorcycles. "My parents insisted I wear it. 'Look sophisticated,' they said. Sophisticated, to visit this dump nunnery." Her dress is a tan one-piece with a turtleneck. She unzips the front until her cleavage shows, and then some more. Now, now, now, the two guys standing by their motorcycles nod, taking enough interest to remove their sunglasses.

"Do these machines ever bite you?"

"Bite? They ain't alive, honey," the one closest to her says. He's built like he lifts weights, like he could pull two of this Japanese girl up from the slough of despond with just one hand.

"You sure?" the Japanese girl asks, cocking her hip and caressing the nearest chrome headlight with metallic blue fingernails.

The two bikers look at one another, then their bikes, both of which throttle up, even though they haven't touched them. Uh, gee, maybe they aren't sure. Could this Japanese sylph have conjured life into their machines?

"Take me for a ride after I sing?"

"Sing?"

"Yes, it's one thing you can do with your mouth." The girl

glances at their crotches, then puckers. The two guys laugh. "I'm singing for the nuns." She motions toward the picnic tables.

A third cab drives by, blaring a horn at an old fart crossing the cobblestone. The Japanese girl flips a bird in such a casual manner that one can't be sure whether she meant it for the old fart carrying the sack of wine or the cab driver.

More cars line up, and some pick-ups. Three noisy motor-scooters. A dog chasing a cat. Two dogs. A woman pushing a stroller, her baby crying as she leans and huffs with the ascent. Four, five birds, mockingbirds by the racket they're making. Isn't it time for them to go to sleep?

Scene five:
Fade in to a bronze plaque on the wall of the maroon brick building. Remember that building? A fingertip presses the plaque, outlining the words *Sisters of Charity.*

"My sis, she's in here." The finger skips from the plaque to pop a dusky brick, as if its operant, a young man, wishes he could knock the wall down. "All this noise—" even as the three motor-scooters buzz by like flying chainsaws, the young man motions across the street, then toward the lake a hundred yards in the distance—"all this noise will drive her over the wall."

The young man's wearing a military uniform. It might be the drab olive in vogue for World War II, but then maybe it's that light tan camouflage used for The Gulf War and Iraq. Hard to tell, 'cause the sun's setting now just when we need it, and no one's bothered to turn on any Klieg lights. The young man is talking to a friend, who's also in uniform. One gets the idea that these two signed up under the buddy plan. Maybe they'll get a bonus instead of two slugs or a lungful of some biochemical disaster. Break a leg, guys.

"Was she the one who used to walk down the street in the middle of the night?"

"That's her."

"No offense, but she was creepy, especially when she sang

those no-word songs."

The young man envisions his father, ape drunk, rubbing his crotch against a chair's back while staring at his only daughter, the young man's sister. "God, over the wall, you poor stupid sad cunt." He smashes the plaque with his fist, which bends him in pain.

The two walk off the set toward a nearby bar. They're not equity guild and their time's up, cameo appearance only.

Scene Six:

The nuns, meanwhile, are shuffling toward the picnic tables. Sister Anne's lost in the middle, between two other nuns, who are also lost in the middle. There's a collective gasp when they turn to see the boys from Mineola Catholic High lining the bridge, ogling downward. Mother Superior smugly announces,

"Sisters, tonight we have a surprise. We're going to have a concert."

And who should be the first to sing but the alligator boy, who's likely squeezed three or four pimples while no poacher was looking. He climbs atop a granite postern and performs, *a cappella,* "Ave Maria." Of course this is what he sings; you wouldn't have him sing "Hey Jude," or "Havin' My Baby," would you?

Even in the dusk—is that sun ever going down?—even in the dusk his skin problem is visible. But I have to tell you that his rendition of "Ave Maria" is a guaranteed tearjerker. We can only thank our lucky stars the choir director isn't Irish. I mean, he won't be having this kid belt out "Danny Boy." Well, the kid's up on the bridge's granite postern, caterwauling away, and it seems like he's forgetting that he's standing over a thirty-five foot drop, the way he keeps shuffling toward the edge. But it's all put-on. The kid's a natural, and even though his voice cracks, he soon has all the nuns in tears. Even the two guys with the motorcycles have turned to listen. Everyone's enthralled, except you-know-who, who sees only one more male and punishes herself with jabs of the crucifix for wishing the kid would tumble off and bust his testicles.

Pan to the stars, even though they're not out. How about a

roseate sunset? No, time's not pushed on that far, either. Anxious, are we? Ready for popcorn? The alligator boy hops down to polite applause and some honking cabby's horn and two barking dogs. Not bad for a first performance. Most of us just have a grim doctor hustling matters along so he can motivate to his next patient—we have him, two bedraggled nurses, and a screaming mother who can't wait for us to finish our little squirming skit—only that serves as audience to our grand entrance.

The nuns, they're squirming, too, because they're hungry. But they have to wait through three more choral efforts. The motorcycle boys have turned back to the Japanese girl, but she's shaking her head, indicating that she has to go to the lake and sing. "I'll be back for that ride, though. If you're sure they don't bite." They blink then laugh, remembering the motorcycles. The dogs are still chasing the cat; the old man's finally made it across the street but drops his wine on seeing the Japanese girl roll her hips; one cab's turned off the ascending road; two more have turned onto it. The couple on the tandem bicycle, who stopped to listen to the alligator boy sing, are mounting up, though they find that starting out mid-hill is too difficult, so they wisely dismount and push the bike uphill after nearly falling. Someone coughs thickly. Maybe it's the woman with the stroller, though I can't see her, and neither can you. Someone in a car flicks a half-smoked cigarette down toward the nuns. Damned cynic. The other street, the one descending, is always barricaded during such open-air dinners, since it's private. This evening, though, a couple on a motor scooter slips through and nearly knock down a server, causing her to drop a tray of overcooked broccoli. Several nuns quietly send a prayer of thanks toward the sky when they see what vegetable has spilled. Above, at least a dozen pigeons cooing and doing their histoplasmotic business ascend at the clatter of breaking dishes.

The high school boys march off, a troop of baboons, one might judge from their guttural snorts and laughs. One boy drops something over the side of the bridge and peers open-mouthed, then scuttles on. It's a condom, which thankfully is taken for a package of gum.

Scene Seven:

The star of love peeps out, silent as usual. Dessert's something the nuns enjoy and do well, so Mother Superior sends three nuns scurrying to make sure the barricade's tightly in place. No more disasters. And, and, and, there's to be a special show. Not to be outdone, the Mineola Girl's Catholic High has sent its prize student, Ms. Aimée Ooka, a Canuck-Japanese hybrid, to sing. She's penned her own inspirational song: it's called, simply, "And That Spells Jesus."

Away from the motorcycle brawn, Ms. Ooka has zipped her tan dress back up to keep her neck warm and her voice in shape. She's now out on the lake, but as young Tommy Daniels recently pointed out to Sister Anne, you shouldn't get upset over time and dates. By that I'm implying that neither should you get upset over space, since Einstein proved the interconnection of the two. So no matter the distance, the nuns, the cab drivers, the motorcyclists, and the old man who's come back from buying another bottle of wine can all hear Ms. Ooka just fine.

"J is for the jo-oy he gi-ives us, E is for each and every day, S stands for— " You, too, can hear her fine, and there's not an entire need to pursue the matter further. But since this is young Aimée's original song, she's added a little twist that she never practiced before her mother or her music coach. She speaks it now, adlibbing in a 1940's blackface: "And X, oh he hoppety along for de Greek *chi* of Christos, baby. De talisman for Christ, 'cause, as dat great man done tol' us"—and here young Aimée bellows out, "I only gots a short ti-ime to di-ie, and I needs to do it right."

Whew. You'd think *that* would get some attention. But there's the same polite applause that was served up for the alligator boy. Except for Sister Anne, whose tears fall into her overcooked broccoli, which is still in front of her because she'd gotten her serving before the accident, and no one can eat dessert until they clean their plate. This is Mother Superior's rule, in consideration of all the starving in distant countries. Ms. Ooka, oblivious to Sister Anne's plate, jumps and waves at the motorcycle boys, running offstage to unzip her dress and head toward them.

You think that maybe we're shortchanging our semi-protagonist, Sister Anne? No, no, it's the masque, the movie, that's shortchanging her—all but forgetting her, really. Hell, she barely needs to be equity, as little as she's been in the film. But she isn't forgetting anything. No, everything is buzzing about her: the motorcycles, the Jap-Canuck girl singing about Christ, the pigeons crapping and flapping, the alligator boy, the limp cold broccoli, the stern Mother Superior, and brainy little Danny-Tommy telling her when Flannery O'Connor died. Even Flannery O'Connor shortchanges Sister Anne—why'd O'Connor have to write all those evil hick characters into existence?

Scene Eight:

So that night, when the nuns go to bed, hearing traffic sounds, breaking bottles, and sirens since they're sleeping outside like Sts. Francis and Clare supposedly did; that night, Sister Anne tosses and weeps. At last she stands, unsteady and wobbling on the air mattress.

"What's wrong, Sister?" another nun asks.

"I've got to piss."

Two nuns who've been embracing—at least we have to believe that's a possibility in Roman Catholic cloisters from what the lesbian press keeps telling us—these two stop short to giggle. "Was that Sister Anne who said *piss*?" they ask in unified amazement.

It was; it *is* Sister Anne, while that machine remains unto her. She runs off the field into the common room where the nunnery keeps computers and one manual typewriter. She turns on a single light, not worrying, for there are no windows to give her away. Even those happy people in that mirthful house across the street can't see me, she thinks. There it is, in the corner. She means the manual typewriter. Its old fashioned, humpedy-bumpedy lines suit her purpose, so she sits, quaintly tucking her habit in like it's a prehensile tail, and she types:

> *Mother Superior:*
> *I'm sorry. It's not just the boys. It's not just men.*
> *It's like the whole world's a movie, jumping around*
> *me, up and down, spinning and whirling, while I'm*
> *tied to a chair and can't even reach my hand to touch*
> *the screen. The sounds and colors leap, but they stop*
> *just short, or they run on by. I'm sorry.*

She pulls the paper from the typewriter and pins it to her habit. She feels the crucifix, but instead of desperately pressing her thumb against Jesus' face as she usually does, she yanks until the cross breaks free of the rosary. She looks at it, sees where she bent it earlier in the day, then walks into the communal bath and forces it head-first into her vagina. There's blood on her hand when she finally pulls away, but she doesn't scream, she only allows herself three mouse-like whimpers, even as its arms cut her uterine wall as she hobbles outside to a shed where last week she noticed a yellow electrical cord they use for outdoor work. It's long and thick and will hold.

She hobbles to the bridge and ties one end of the cord around the thick postern that the alligator boy had stood on, though she can't imagine how, for it's transformed into a large concrete ball the size of a pocked globe. There's China, there's Japan—mission territory. There's her hometown. She can see her prick-of-a-father's face, smell his sour beer breath. Inhaling, she wraps the other end of the yellow outdoor cord around her neck. There's no moon, she notices. In the distance, a siren sounds. Nearby, a bottle breaks. She climbs atop the wall, then the post's concrete ball, looking down on the picnic tables. And then she jumps.

A kaleidoscope of colors and stars press against her eyes. And she's right: they pass her quickly by. The force of the fall ejects the crucifix from her vagina. It lands with a bloody clink on the cobblestone below. The camera could focus on that, couldn't it, as a confused sign of rebirth? It could, but Sister Anne's body is twitching and scraping against the bridge above, doing a macabre dance that's entranced the camera's operator—is that you?—and then everything stills and it's entirely too late for rebirth.

Final Scene:

An hour later, Ms. Aimée Ooka will ride underneath on the back of a motorcycle and scream. They'll stop and the weightlifter will scale the wall's granite outcroppings like Mighty Joe Young to ease Sister Anne down. As he does, Aimée, barefoot, will step on the bloody crucifix, hop away and look up into the darkness of the sister's many folds of robe as they billow with the descent. Aimée will see all in a sort of vision, even as she and the other cyclist mutely receive the dead nun into their arms. This gesture stands the closest to love—other than her younger brother's frightened whimpers—that Sister Anne has ever come in her life. Since she jumped only one hour ago, can't some single cell in her pre-frontal lobe remain alert enough to luxuriate in this miniature Pièta? Can't little Tommy Daniels be right about the unimportance of time?

No. This masque is done.

The Secret Life of Atheists

After two indulgent hours at a café, Jean-Paul Sartre and Albert Camus went strolling down a hot Paris street. This happened close enough after World War II's end that both the irony and the hope of a clear-skied afternoon tugged them. Albert looked up to spot a *fille* of about 18 ripe years leaning to water potted daisies on an iron balcony. She smiled broadly—to render matters quaintly—but he'd drunk too much red wine to care, so he waved her off even as daisy-water dripped on his forehead. Jean-Paul, however, gazed up into her grey eyes and beheld a vision worthy of Saint Joan of Arc: a virgin offering a dull silver chalice in one hand, a swash of golden sunlight in her other. He stumbled, Albert caught him by the arm, and the *fille* laughed. "May the Immaculate Virgin Mother show mercy to you both!" she called, placing a daisy in her dark, dark hair, then laughing again as the two regained composure and continued their stroll.

One block later, a car screeched onto the curb and the two philosophers had to jump to avoid it—*Mon* damned *Dieu!* Albert sobered considerably, gawking at a tumbling garbage can spewing empty wine bottles and half-full cans of suspiciously *Wermacht-*grey paint. They flipped off the drunken driver, who was too busy hitting his head against the steering wheel to notice anything but the grey paint spattered on his windshield.

Oddly, the image of the black-haired girl watering the daisies revisited Albert. "Why . . . why would a whore implore the Immaculate Virgin Mother's mercy on us?" he asked Jean-Paul.

"Bad Faith," Jean-Paul replied without hesitation. It was a concept he'd been working over.

Albert thought the response a joke and laughed. "*Ah oui.* Maybe she learned that from the American GI's. Or maybe from Joe Stalin." Immediately, he regretted mentioning either, for he didn't want to get into politics with Jean-Paul. They'd been arguing enough over that lately, though not—praise heaven and its non-loquacious saints—at the café they just left. Albert whiffed and smelled American whiskey—from the drunken driver? Then, not a dozen steps later, he spotted her, hips beating time like the many death rattles he'd heard in the past hard years of Nazi occupation and the too-recent horrific French backlash against supposed collaborators.

"*Mon Dieu.* Simone," he warned Jean-Paul.

Jean-Paul instinctively grabbed his crotch and turned into a shopkeeper's recessed doorway to stare at a window display of naked dolls. The shopkeeper was squatting in the display case, busily fluffing doll clothes. When she saw Jean-Paul's shadow and turned to see him holding his privates, she wagged her finger fiercely, finally butting her head against the glass.

"Did she see me?" Jean-Paul asked his friend Albert, ignoring the shopkeeper as she protectively gathered the nude dolls unto her overabundant breasts. Albert was considering that this shopkeeper surely must have been a collaborator to have maintained breasts that large throughout the *boche* occupation.

"I fear so." Seeing Albert's mouth move and hearing his voice through the open transom, the shopkeeper turned her hazel eyes and fine dark lashes to him, pushing him backward as effectively as the car had moments before. "But maybe not." Albert's proclamation covered both Simone and the dismissal of his suspicions about the lovely shopkeeper after gazing into her even lovelier eyes. "Say, *mon ami*, why don't you ask this shopkeeper to let us in? She should be reopening for the afternoon anyway." Inhaling deeply, Albert glanced at the shopkeeper, who again was glaring at Jean-Paul, who appeared to have lapsed into philosophical reverie. Not bad faith, but bad timing, Albert mused, for he could hear Simone's post-war high heels bitterly clacking the sidewalk.

What Jean-Paul was thinking:

He'd noted that two of the dolls gathered in the shopkeeper's arms kept their eyes closed, while the third kept its eyes open. *Ah la*, he pondered, is this our human life, *comme* these tiny dolls? Tilt us one way and our being opens with an affirming *Oui*? Tilt us another, and a sleepy *Non* drizzles from our consciousness? Being and non? Being and nothing? Being and Nothingness? *Lord help us then.*

This was perhaps the last known prayer Jean-Paul ever uttered, save for whenever Simone drove him to his metaphorical knees.

Simone, as if obeying a Swiss clock-maker's mechanical cue, shouted, "*Vous!*"

This is not good, both men realized. With that guttural *vous* she's not using the plural equivalent of the quaint Southern American "Y'all." No way. She's refusing to *tutoyer* either of us.

"You," Simone continued in the husky voice so popular with female French cabaret singers. "Why have you been simpering about town, avoiding me? I saw you back there flirting with that black-haired *fille!*"

This preternatural insight of women always amazed the two men, and they'd discussed it over many a cup of café latte that nearly always changed into not so miraculous red wine. For Jean-Paul this feminine trait would gargle upward to seed several works, from *Nausea* to *No Exit*. But it also secreted a choking phlegm for his grand psychological/philosophical *opus magnum* in the making, for if women truly did possess an imbedded supernatural or even preternatural sixth sense, just where would that leave the nothingness he so handily envisioned as the wellspring of all human minds, regardless of sex? *Ah la . . . maybe les femmes are not human*, he theorized. As Simone glared at him he blinked, his body echoing the thought, recalling how he'd tripped over a swell of nothingness leaning over a balcony two blocks back.

"He didn't really say anything to the girl, it was just the

dripping water and the daisy—"

"Al-bare, do not defend him. You're just like every other man, coming to the aid of a brother prick on the make."

Albert winced, but not from what you might think, that is not from the insult to his moral standing, nor the shrinking of it into a base sexual appendage. No, he winced at Simone's pronunciation of his name in the perfectly Parisian manner, albeit protracted for the situation. *Al-bare. Al-Bear.* He could never hear it without thinking of the two English equivalents. What good had a multilingual education gotten him, if these were the results: The ability to read a depressing Southern writer named Faulkner and his dusty-hot novels, and then the theft of his very own name, his very own identity. *Lord save me*, he thought. A fate worse than Sisyphus's.

Jean-Paul, meanwhile, started to fumble his pipe from a vest pocket but thought better of it, considering the proximity of Simone. Recently, she'd complained about the acrid smell from the Turkish latakia tobacco he'd grown fond of. So he let the pipe rest and reached to brush her upper arm in a doting manner.

"No *fille*, no *fille*. My eyes," he hoarsely whispered, "stray only to you."

"Oh give it a break!" This Americanism came not from any of the trio, but from the shopkeeper kneeling inside, who heard Jean-Paul's voice magnify as it drifted through the upper vented transom she'd opened in search of pre-air-conditioning airflow.

With sudden awareness, Simone widened her eyes at the sight of the three dolls almost suckling the woman's abundant breasts. *My God*, she thought, seeing herself miniaturized in the brown-haired doll with ringlets crowning its head. *Mon Dieu, but am I not as beautiful as that doll? Do I not deserve the unrivalled attention of not just one, but of two great men? No common fille should–*. She laughed hoarsely, as if she'd been smoking Jean-Paul's Turkish tobacco—of course she *had* been smoking it, staying stuffed beside him in tiny upstairs bedrooms and in countless smoky cafes during rain. *Mon Dieu, jealousy: the eternal feminine trap. Give it a break*, she thought, echoing the shopkeeper, who stood to vigorously motion Simone inside.

"You two, y'all wait here." Simone underlined the Southernism to dish out some jealousy to Jean-Paul, for she'd read the Faulkner fellow at Albert's insistence.

Giving Jean-Paul an evil eye, the shopkeeper unlatched the door and led Simone to her L-shaped display counter, which leaned against an oaken stairway, which itself leaned against the shop's green-slatted wooden wall. Maybe in support? Why not? Everything else in Europe seemed to teeter from the vast war's aftermath.

As the door swung closed, Albert watched the two women. Well, he watched their rear ends, and remembering those hazel eyes he did a quick reassessment of the shopkeeper, who bore not only abundant breasts but a luscious derriere. *Mon Dieu*, he thought, *damn that Austrian fellow. Could he be right about human motivation? Does it thrust no deeper than cigars and caves, daggers and spoons?*

"Hasn't one Austrian done enough damage to the world already?" he asked Jean-Paul, who was back to pondering the half-dozen remaining dolls and their unblinking eyes.

"Eh?" Jean-Paul said.

"Freud and Hitler. The two have left the world in a shambles."

Jean-Paul blinked.

This blinking was all that many people had gotten from him lately, and it was what was bothering Simone so much these days, at least this was Albert's analysis of the affair. It wasn't the damned pipe tobacco like Jean-Paul thought that was setting Simone on edge, though admittedly the mix did stink up to high-angel heaven and down to low-swine hell. Albert grimaced. "Come on, Jean-Paul, let's step inside. That shopkeeper has eyes for me."

"Hell lies in the eyes of the other," Jean-Paul warned.

"Heaven," Albert countered.

"Heaven? Even if she were an angel, she couldn't very well

dance on a pinhead. Too top-heavy."

"Soulful, full of milk-love," Albert countered. "With the precious toes of a guardian angel." Albert, a connoisseur of toes, had glimpsed the woman's bare feet before she exited the display window.

Metaphysicians, note well: thus transpired one of the more theological discussions the two friends ever held. But back upon earth, the inside of the shop smelled—to Albert anyway—of candles and incense, and it reminded him of the cathedral he'd hidden in after breaking into a Vichy sub-police station to steal weapons to kill Nazis. To Jean-Paul, the shop smelled like Turkish latakia. But then perhaps everything smelled that way, to Jean-Paul.

"Ah," Simone said, turning to the approaching men, but speaking to the shopkeeper. "You were right. They couldn't resist coming in."

"What did I tell you, darling? The weaker, the second sex."

Albert heard only the very last 's' word and shook his head. Freud again. It was enough to push an atheist to religion. In fact, one last word led to another, and soon enough Albert asked the shopkeeper if she cared to dine with the three of them that night.

"Better than that," she said. "Why don't we eat upstairs where I live?" Her hazel eyes indicated the second floor above them. "My father runs a farm and has just slaughtered a fine sheep for me."

None of the trio had eaten mutton since before the war, so they were more than agreeable. At six that evening they showed up with several bottles of Haut Medoc, which Albert uncorked. Jean-Paul and Simone were gazing about the swank upper apartment with its two fireplaces, two balconies, and a fine six-burner gas stove. Albert, however, gazed only at the distance between the shopkeeper's breasts. Within that mystical distance rested an odd pendant.

"Joan," he sighed—her name was Joan, and he thought of France's blessed Joan of Arc. "Joan . . . that necklace you're wearing is . . . ?"

"Amber." She twisted so that her blouse revealed a dark

aureole, for she was using the extended shortages spread over post-war Europe as an excuse not to burn, but to disregard her bras.

Albert wasted no time in bringing Joan a glass of wine and even less time in taking the amber pendant, warm from her breasts and/or the oven, into his palm. "Whatever's trapped inside looks like a Buddha, one of the laughing ones, I mean."

"Let me see." Simone came to Joan's aid in case Albert's hands started roaming too early in the evening. She was surprised at the pendant's weight and became curious as to what Albert had said about the Buddha. "No, Albert, I think it's more like Kali, the Hindu goddess of death and war and love and hate and . . ."

Jean-Paul moved in on the act, though he didn't dare cup the pendant in his hand, not after the grey-eyed Joan of Arc *fille* on the balcony earlier in the day. So he studied it in Simone's hand, making sure to caress her fingers as he did—and to doubly avoid both the hazel eyes and cherry-dark aureoles of The Other. Momentarily he considered: Could nipples and aureoles be as damaging as eyes? He decided that Al-bare was right: the Austrian fellow Freud had done enough theoretic damage already.

Both Simone and Albert, patiently studying their friend's face, were ready for him to claim that the bug trapped inside the amber resembled the hammer and sickle, for Jean-Paul had been lathering communism on rather heavily for the past month despite that asshole Stalin, whom Albert figured must have been secretly born in Austria.

But Jean-Paul surprised them:

"A country Crucifix. I saw one like it as a child. A crude, contorted Jesus, legs broken, arms akimbo, gaze eruptively sad."

"Have some wine," Albert offered. Communism was bad enough; if Jean-Paul reverted to Christianity, their entire friendship would dissolve.

"It's all those things to me—Kali, Buddha, Jesus," Joan offered. She opened the oven door and the aroma of Daddy's sacrificial mutton spiraled out.

"All?" Simone barked, incredulous, non-credulous.

"And more," Joan replied. How many Frenchies have hazel eyes, Albert wondered. Did she have maybe some Basque in her? His spine shivered as she continued speaking, "Much more. I believe in . . . visions."

"Like your namesake?" Simone reached for the wine Albert had neglected to hand her, though he'd at least been polite enough to pour four glasses.

"Oh no, I'm named after the American actress Joan Crawford. My mother's American. . . ."

They're taking over the world, Albert concluded. *Well, maybe they'll do better than the Austrians anyway.* Though he figured the atomic bomb didn't bode well as an American starting block.

". . . So my visions are more like the Hollywood movies. You know, a happy ending for everyone." Joan sighed and put down her wine glass to fold her hands palm in palm before her ample breasts. "Brotherhood." She glanced at Simone. "And sisterhood," she added. "World peace."

They stared blankly at her. Though Miss America had been modeling swimsuits at the Paris airport just last year, the actual pageant hadn't made its way to Europe or the trio would have caught Joan's sarcasm. As it was, she had to back out by saying,

"Well, I just figured that 'world peace' would go over better with three renowned atheists than what I really believe. . . ."

The three leaned.

"A pan-religion. Like Pan the Greek god, all-encompassing. A brain is wider than the sky."

"Ah," Albert affirmed, being quick on the uptake, even though the Belle of Amherst hadn't made her way to Europe either. "Ah," he said again. "Spinoza, an ur-God."

Dinner was served, and Daddy's sacrificial lamb—or at least one of its legs—was picked clean. After the third bottle of wine and dessert, an almond chocolate-cream pastry, Albert wound up pawing the amber pendant, though perhaps that had not been his original Freudian intent. Feeling the room's heat, Joan suddenly held the amber before her face, her eyes widening with horror. She turned to Albert.

"Avoid sports cars," she said. "At all costs. Avoid!"

While Simone nodded gravely at this dark feminine insight—all women are Cassandras, she thought—the two men consulted one another with raised eyebrows. More female mumbo-jumbo? The infamous female sixth sense? By heaven, things *could* have been worse, Albert concluded. Hitler and the Eva Braun bitch could have spawned a girl-child down in the bunkers. Or the kook Jung could have stayed pals with Freud and married Freud's daughter Anna to conjure web upon web of archetypal potty-training. Lord save us. *Mon Dieu, mon Dieu.*

Night strengthened; wills weakened. The time arrived for boys to be boys and girls to be girls. The couples separated, Simone and Jean-Paul hoofing to her apartment eight blocks away, while Albert and Joan wandered onto the back balcony, which overlooked Joan's enclosed garden. Below, Albert could make out a statue of Saint Francis. Italy via America into France. Where would it end? Something was crawling in the statue's left upturned palm, snuffling through the grain that palm held. He suspected it was a black Norway rat, so he willingly looked up to the sky as Joan pushed him down on the blankets she'd spread on the balcony. As she cooed and coaxed him from a wine reverie and fed him into herself, he noticed a constellation he'd never seen before. Keeping his eyes open, he swayed into the rhythm Joan set. As her vigor increased, she dropped her French sweet-nothings and took up an American dialect he couldn't quite make out. Praising Mickey Mouse, for all he knew. Her hair, which had perched in a strangely coifed spiral during dinner, now fell in wisps across his eyes.

"*Mon Dieu!*" he exclaimed as he climaxed, for the constellation had winked, like a great all-seeing eye.

At approximately the same time eight blocks away, Simone laid down a bed of pillows on her balcony. To make up for the *fille* and for the damned Turkish tobacco and the ever-increasing absent-minded blinks, she wanted to get Jean-Paul on his knees, she wanted him to wash her feet with his tears and his beard.

But he didn't have a beard. And it was only Germans who cried in their beer, them and poor whites from Faulkner's Southern states of America. And she and Jean-Paul had drunk wine all night anyway, not beer, to top the list of objections.

So . . . back and forth, back and forth, in the egalitarian way they compromised on, a he-thrust, a she-thrust, their tempo increasing like a sultry jazz tune until upon reaching their joint petit mort they both exclaimed, "*Mon Dieu!*"

Once more, that strange constellation, that great all-seeing eye, winked. —Or rather, did it, like a willful, hermetic New England crone, dole a single approving nod?

Highway One, Revisited

Sooner or later, it's a dead end, you might philosophically assert. You might say this even as you hear glass shatter ahead, even as you later come upon a six pack of beer bottles mapped across that highway like gaseous stellar matter novaed across the Crab Nebula.

Sooner or later, you register numbly.

And sometime on, you could tire from the morning heat and know well that somewhere on that street a man or a woman (sex rolls unimportantly for those fates, you realize) had been killed during the night. That a babe had been born while a mother had been ambulance-whisked. You could know this with a surety born of length rather than logic.

You: I say *you* for fear of saying *we* or *I*, for fear of intruding upon your fantasy. I want you to see or do what you want to see or do upon this street, upon Highway One, vagabond kin of tourism's A-1-A. For where A-1-A froths life and glitter, One mires grime and sweat in its stinking damned tar, tar kept from the charm of torpedo rays, Man-o-Wars, and moray eels nestled in clear, azure waters. Kept from that oceany romance and ribboned instead across a speeding realm of whores and queers and dented pick-ups and recycled Northern city busses.

But I give too much of myself away. It is you who walk that hot, tired asphalt toward that hot, tired horizon.

Again: away from the ocean. Finish. And into the flatly faded pink and green and chalk-blue stucco houses that squat over south Florida. There.

You could, should you be so inclined, walk upon Highway One from Harry's Banana Farm, home of hot pepperoncinis and icy cold beer, to, say, Key West, or, say, some vague point north. But the North is so unhip that you want to just leave it up there: north. Just know that you could walk farther in a northerly fashion than you would ever care to.

And you, or you and your mate (or we, if I might be so bold) could trip through strip shopping centers with tiny stucco bars and tiny stucco karate dojos, through those and palmettos and dirty looks and tourists and cops—you could trip through all that ménage while travelling this highway, this Kerouacian dream of American culture.

Along the road, babe, you and me, babe.

"Need a ride?"

"No thanks."

And you would walk on, a bit stiffly, a bit alertly, for you would know, whatever your sex, that what he wanted to give you wasn't a ride, but a ride. Can you dig?

Axiom: Better to lie under a palmetto than to be taken for a ride. And palmettos do house rattlesnakes, no shit.

Well, say you might start at Harry's, at say a reasonable hour, at say ten in the morning. And say you wouldn't want a pepperoncini just then, but that a Bloody Mary might serve as just the right constitutional. The bartender (a she in the morning) would splash it out, happily out, she being accustomed to straightening bleary eyes from the stench of the previous night. A goddess, glistening in the morning sun. And you would drop that goddess a sizely tip, wouldn't you? Then we (sorry) you would talk with your friend (lover) about the weather, I mean about the sunrise. If you were a tourist, you would swear that the sunrise is different, more spectacular along Highway One than anywhere else in the country. But you couldn't be a tourist, or you'd be on Highway A-1-A, wouldn't you? Not on this surly, ragged Highway One. So, maybe you're one of the state's newly acquired residents, or even a native, and you would say, "Damn, it's going to be a hot one." Then you would get down to business, either way.

"Which way?" You'd look to yours, hoping for a bold response.

"I don't know, which way?" yours would answer.

Perhaps, if you were lucky, the bartender would overhear and would tell you and yours of a zoo up in West Palm or a carnival down in Lantana. Never in Lake Worth, for the people in Lake Worth, the bartender and all her kin, want you to move on. They've seen your kind before, friend.

Misunderstanding her intent, you might feel obligated to leave an even bigger tip or stay for another Bloody Mary. And soon it would be time for those wonderful pepperoncinis that inhabit that gallon jar stuck before the mirror. It would be time, because it's a little before noon and the local restaurant workers are coming in to stretch their day into as much oblivion as they can before they have to wait on people like you during the talons of night.

Or hey, maybe I've got you all wrong.

But you'd stay, just because some life had started swimming before you, and you never could drag yourself from an aquarium.

So the restaurateurs would talk about those sons of bitches they wait on, or that little blonde cunt or that sweet-lipped guy with the bulging crank or that nervous bastard they work for who's always dropping cigarette ashes in the food and ruining their tips. They might even talk about how hot it is already. And they would hold their beer cans to their foreheads and shiver with the cool.

Your cheeks are getting a bit ticklish now, you tell yours. And yours replies that the both of you should have eaten something besides those goddamned pepperoncinis. And you should have.

"The beach, it's just two miles from here," the bartender might say. But she doesn't really care, because she gets off soon and Harry or Harry Junior will have to take over and stare at you.

Tourists, you believe you hear the restaurateurs think or whisper.

But maybe I've got you all wrong.

The hell with the zoo and the carnival and the beach, you say to yours, because I've got you all wrong. And you and yours switch to beer. Busch. And you hold your beer cans to your foreheads and shiver with the cool.

And who can blame you, because it's so goddamned hot.

There was a kid, you hear, *got all cut up into pieces,* you hear, *some queer kid cut up into pieces last night and dripped into a Dempster-Dumpster not two hundred yards from here. Dripped like sour bacon,* you hear, *two legs there, an arm here, and no damned head nowhere. What the hell they want the damned kid's head for?* you hear.

"Jesus," you say.

And yours grips the beer can tightly and orders another,

"Jesus," yours finally agrees.

And for a moment—a slick, scary moment that slips over itself—you think you ought to get the hell out of there. I mean, really out of there.

But it passes. It passes like some son-of-a-bitch train that you can't even see, but only hear. Wheeeeeeeeeeeeeeeeeeeeeooooooooooo ooooh. Like some son-of-a-bitch train whistling and huffing in a great sweat through the hot air somewhere like it knows where it's going and like it has to deliver a great rush to get there.

So instead of leaving, you stucco your stomach with more of those hot things that look sad and green like the pickled penis of some queer kid. With a double order of those sweet Club Crackers, please. You've over-tipped again, so the bartender, she isn't as anxious for you to leave as she was.

"You two from up north?" she asks. Not by way of being stupid, but just that there isn't much else to say to two strangers if you don't want to talk about the heat.

"Yeah," one of you answers.

And she puts the food down in front of you after wiping the counter good and clean.

Good and by god clean.

Suddenly, you think you've got a new jump on life. I mean,

you don't leave, you don't talk about the goddamned sunrise or beach or zoo anymore, you don't even talk about the heat or care what the damned restaurateurs think because you're some-damned body now.

And it's time to make some plans.

"Which way?" you ask lightly of yours.

"I don't know, which way?" yours says, sorting each word through a tightly bitten knuckle, sorting each word while trying to ignore the blood and grime and alcohol and pain and saliva and sweat—trying to ignore all that; trying instead to concentrate on some stupid damned Florida alligator's skull cutely stuffed with some stupid damned beer tabs that glitter among those once-proud teeth just like the shattered glass glittered over that stupid highway outside some time back.

"I don't know . . . which way?" yours repeats with a shiver.

Morality Play

One Tuesday in June, Saul Gibson awoke to the striated song of an angry mockingbird. Twisting his torso to see the open bedroom window, he realized that last night's air must have turned uncommonly warm after his wife came home from play rehearsal. Unwinding his legs from hers, he heard a blues note that didn't come from the bird, so he shifted onto his elbows to discover his wife Lyra had six steel guitar strings stretched from her collarbone to her pubis. She was sleeping soundly and showed no discomfort, so he plucked the top string. It rang a high, clear E: *Mi*. The mockingbird imitated it poorly. He then plucked the lowest, and it rang just as clearly, two octaves lower: **Mi**. The mockingbird was silent; evidently this low E was out of its range.

Lyra gave a contented sigh. Saul took it on faith that her intervening strings were in tune, so he got out of bed and eyed the room's air conditioner, for the day was already working into heat. After turning the AC unit on, he tried to close the window, but the mockingbird flew straight at him, cracking a pane. The bird bashed another pane, then perched in a weeping willow and yelped, eyeing Saul balefully. Backing off, Saul raised his palms, leaving the window open about five inches.

Lyra awoke and stretched, a cacophony of notes and chords sounding as she did. Since she paid them little mind Saul decided that the guitar strings shouldn't concern him, either. After all, tiring of work's grind he'd been compulsively shopping on E-bay for the last month and a half, and guitar brands were daily racing through his head: Martin; Guild; Gretsch; his namesake, Gibson; Taylor; Alvarez; Goya. Maybe the whole shebang had osmosed over to his wife of five years. Or maybe that prideful thought reversed matters: maybe it was her name, Lyra, suggested by an oddball grandmother, which inspired both her change and his, since "Lyra" meant *lute* in Latin. Or maybe it was Lyra's very own psyche that instigated her anatomical change. Anatomy following spirituality? He glanced back as her right hand innocently sifted a rhapsodic arpeggio, which the mockingbird, now on the windowsill, answered. Saul walked downstairs, scratching his navel as he retrieved the morning paper.

Before breakfast—which he always cooked, letting his more imaginative wife cook dinner—he called upstairs to ask Lyra how many pancakes she wanted. Plucking her strings from the top step, she answered, *Do, do, re, so*, leaving the *so* a bit ragged, but then it was twenty till seven in the morning. *Four?* Saul mused, recounting the notes and wondering why she might want that many pancakes. Lyra had remained a petite hundred and eleven pounds over the last four years, though they'd both gained weight their first year of marriage from grazing on fudge cake, and maybe too a couple of pounds had been added after moving across country to their present township of Ur just last year.

When she came into the kitchen, something, perhaps the ticking of the clock, perhaps the shifting of her hips as she fetched breakfast plates, reminded Saul that she'd attended play rehearsal last night while he hadn't. His face fell, for he'd missed rehearsal for the umpteenth time. He really wasn't even sure what piece the local theater group was performing, other than some off-the-wall revival by the Frenchman Voltaire. No, not Moliere, he constantly told his almost bright co-workers—Voltaire, the guy who wrote *Candide*. Forgetting the play, he served Lyra four pancakes. As he did, she shyly nudged a chartreuse 5 x 6 card toward him:

> Mr. Gibson:
>
>> *You have missed or left sixteen rehearsals,*
>> *seventeen including last night's dress rehearsal.*

Reluctantly, we are going to have to fine you forty-five écu. We are calling a second dress rehearsal on your behalf tomorrow night. No doubt you will grace us with your attendance.

When Saul first saw the note his eyes hit upon the word "Reluctantly" and he hoped he was being dropped from the cast, though the social consequences of that left him nervous. But no such luck. Instead, he was being fined these forty-five "écu's" –whatever they were. Some cute French phrasing to do with the play, he conjectured.

Lyra was no help; she pointed to the chartreuse note and plucked, *Do, ra, so, ti, do,* scat-singing the notes too.

"Ra?" Saul asked, thinking of the Sun God.

Ra, she repeated. *Ra, Re, Ri.*

"Ah, flats and sharps. Brilliant, Lyra."

Her six strings vibrated in appreciation. Saul noticed a sounding hole enlarging where her belly button used to be. He could almost see quarter and half notes dancing inside. He looked to her mouth: she could eat, so surely she could still talk. Maybe she just didn't want to. Maybe the beauty of the stringed notes rendered talking superfluous.

Keeping the chartreuse card between them on the table, they ate pancakes, listening to the mockingbird that sounded as if it had flown into their bedroom upstairs. Saul spilled syrup on the card. He didn't like the director of the play, who thought himself a godlike figure, even God the father, with his huge white beard. *Patriarchy's out,* Saul wanted to yell on the first night's rehearsal. Instead, he'd stepped outside, lit a cigar, and watched the sun setting. Saul slowed eating, for the chartreuse card absolutely repelled the syrup, beading it. This figured: nothing could get through.

While one couldn't say it was obligatory for voting age citizens in the township of Ur to participate in at least one community play per year, one couldn't say it *wasn't* obligatory either. Saul glanced at the chartreuse card and its forty-five écu fine. Lyra's fingers skittered from the pancakes to her guitar strings. Had she grown fret markers too? It appeared that way, for eight pearl fleurs-de-lis rose upon her torso, as if she were a handmade Yairi from Japan. Catching his gaze, she played a few measures of a bluegrass song, "Rock-salt and nails." Did this indicate that his punishment for missing dress rehearsal would be more severe than he thought? Well, at least she hadn't strummed "The Long Black Veil," "Tom Dooley," or any number of dreary hanging songs. Damn it, he didn't want to act in the stupid play no matter what the consequences. He wanted to listen to Lyra strum.

"I'm going to work," he said, carrying their plates to the sink.

Lyra plucked out "Maid of Constant Sorrow," so he kissed her twice. He momentarily wondered what her office co-workers would think of the guitar strings. Likely she'd wear a large blouse to cover them. And she was in computers, so she really needn't talk with anyone all that much anyway.

Ur was a bedroom community that prided itself on setting the cutting edge for both computers and lifestyles. Hence, it sponsored fifteen community plays per year with the fidelity that many towns sponsored football and cheerleading. And Ur boasted three Unitarian churches, a dozen New-Age chapels, five espresso and two kava-kava bars. Despite these statistics, upon hearing the mockingbird as he opened the front door—it had moved into a neighbor's oak—Saul stopped halfway in his move to kiss Lyra and instead threw up his arms, causing her to spill her coffee. He pointed at her six strings and shouted, "What about the Voltaire play?! What will you do?"

Lyra's eyes widened in panic.

* * *

Saul missed the second dress rehearsal too—not completely on purpose, for he'd stopped at an espresso bar and logged onto the Internet in an effort to discover what brand of guitar Lyra had become. Rather than the Yairi he'd first imagined, he was now almost certain she was a Gibson Hummingbird, for the last thing he'd seen when she spilled her coffee was the start of a pick guard on her left abdomen, one which featured a string of flowers and what looked like a bird's beak. The Internet search intrigued him so much that when he finally looked up it was past ten. Even with a dress rehearsal, they'd be done by the time he could drive to the auditorium, so he simply went home to bed.

When Lyra came home from rehearsal he barely awoke. And in the morning when he got out of bed upon hearing the same damned mockingbird, she'd already left for work, so he had no idea how matters had gone at the play. Her note on the kitchen table did seem unduly terse, saying she had "urgent matters at the office." Still, he stayed hopeful she'd managed to wing it last night, for she was nothing if not inventive. He might be the one who vocally protested societal pressure, but her protests came through inner change, where it mattered. After all, wasn't she the one who transformed into a guitar? What an ingenious solution! He himself was only buying, consuming, and avoiding.

At work, Saul encountered glaring faces everywhere, and they served to dampen his exclamatory optimism. Little vindictive annoyances were placed in his way throughout the day: The coffee pot was either empty or unplugged and cold when he walked to it; someone was smoking a cigarette around his cubicle nearly every half hour and once marijuana in a cigar, though the entire building was subject to a no-smoking policy, not to mention drugs. At lunch, the mushroom soup he was served had soured. When he took it back for a hamburger, which tasted nearly raw, he threw that away too, going lunchless. That afternoon horseflies, yellow jackets, and a black widow spider found their way into his cubicle as if fed through ductwork or tossed over the partitions. His desk light flickered. His computer lost power four times, and his air-conditioning vent emitted a vile smell of rotting flesh—the hamburger? The paper shredder jammed when he used it. His papers had honey on them, though he hated honey and never ate it. Finally, at a quarter to five, after a day of near silence from his co-workers, a paper airplane dropped onto his desk.

135 écu

Another Dress Rehearsal!

This was written on its two wings, in splotchy blood red. Had the fine tripled? Angry, he stomped to the restroom, where he discovered a fret instead of a belly button. Lifting his shirt covertly, he discovered two more frets. He was evidently working in a pattern reversed from Lyra's, though the end result would likely be the same. It appeared that he was growing two f-holes about his ribs as opposed to a single sounding hole at his belly button. The paper airplane was gone when he came back, but his cubicle smelled of vinegar.

Happy to leave work, Saul stopped at an ATM to withdraw three hundred dollars, what he figured would surely cover the forty-five, or even hundred thirty-five écu fine. But his account had been frozen. He ran to the front of the bank, which closed at five-thirty. A young teller with red, high cheeks and equally red hair snapped the blinds shut in his face. When he banged on the entrance, her hand emerged between slats to twist like an adder and point to the hours of operation. This teller, he'd often noticed, had to use a huge purse full of make-up to cover bruises where her husband hit her. Now her bracelet scraped the plate glass in one last coiling gesture toward the closing time. As her hand disappeared he spotted bruises on her wrist the size of fingerprints.

Driving home, he felt his neck being pulled to the right as he gathered change and occasional dollar bills from various receptacles in the car, hoping to scrape enough together to cover the stupid fine. He itched his chest and heard a low E, **Mi.** So he truly was growing a guitar's fingerboard just like Lyra. By the time he turned onto his street, his neck had straightened as the high E string tightened. By the time he put his key in the back door, all six strings were in place. It was pleasurable to feel them tuning.

He paused before opening the door. He could hear Lyra; that is, he could hear lively classical music . . . Vivaldi? . . . playing on strings. Several times, his own strings vibrated in sympathy. Suddenly the music stopped and there was weeping. Saul opened the door and rushed in to find Lyra at the kitchen table, a demitasse of espresso on her right, a glass of red wine on her left. She was weeping so heavily that she didn't hear him and jumped when he placed a hand on her shoulder. A chartreuse card lay between the wine glass and the espresso. He did a double-take, for he'd carried his card to the office, wanting advice, though no one had been willing to talk with him about work, weather, or even sports, much less a forty-five écu fine. He looked at the new card on the table and saw it wasn't addressed to him:

Ms. Gibson:

Reluctantly, we must fine you forty-five écu. Your voice has turned entirely unacceptable for the play, despite your implicit promises to care for it as a tenure of Ur township. If we understood you correctly last night at rehearsal—it seems entirely possible we did not, considering your new "voice"—your offer of holding up placards hardly constitutes an acceptable solution to speaking lines. We expect you tonight at the last extra dress rehearsal necessitated by . . . well of course you very well know who necessitated it. If somehow your voice has mended, the fine may be lessened.

He reached to wipe a tear from Lyra's hazel eyes. Then he sat and the two of them practiced scales, trading step-ups and competing in tempo. Forty minutes before it was time to leave for the rehearsal, Saul started in on "Pavane for a Dead Princess." Lyra giggled and joined in duet. Afterwards, she worked into a Rachmaninoff torch song, "O Cease Thy Singing, Maiden Fair," and Saul interpolated a violin obbligato on his own fretwork. A jazzy "Malagueña" duet came next. He slid off his left shoe and kept time on her bare foot. Shoulder to shoulder they played. Tossing her head in a laugh, Lyra intoned a steamy Jimmy Smith tune, "Got My Mojo Workin'." Saul licked her ear while providing a pumping, peppery bass accompaniment. She was rotating her hips to achieve the bending bluesy notes. When she reached to play a high rift on his E and B strings, he felt a vigour he hadn't felt since he was twenty, a vigour worthy of the extra British vowel. He and Lyra meshed splendidly, as if a single, lovely twelve-string Gibson guitar.

They arrived twenty minutes late for the last dress rehearsal. On the drive over, Lyra had done her best to explain the Voltaire play, but all Saul connected with was some Muslim prince analyzing Christianity. It was rather difficult to understand her plucking when she talked about outside matters, he had to admit, even with sharps and flats. Moreover, they'd wound up robbing their coin collection of half-, silver-, and the new gold dollars, and the resultant clanking of four hundred coins with each pothole the car hit did nothing to aid communication. Saul envisioned throwing the whole sack at the snooty teller.

"Late!" the director screamed as they walked in.

"Late!" the cast onstage yelled.

Saul saw the redheaded teller, her right cheek puttied against the glare of Klieg lights. He and Lyra hurried toward the stage but were instead surrounded by five members of the International Spa Youth, who herded them into nearby auditorium seats.

"Because of you two," the director yelled while stroking his long white beard, "we've had to make a last minute change of plays." He paused for dramatic effect, as stage folk always do. "We have resurrected, if you will, a French morality play named *Rhinocéros*. I myself have improved the stage directions and dialogue."

"*Naturellement*," Lyra said.

Saul started in surprise at her voice, but one of the International Spa Youth cuffed her head, sending her low E string into convulsion.

"Silence!" the director shouted, causing Lyra to grab and muffle her string.

The cast deserted the stage and the house lights were dimmed, while the stage lights flickered, allowing time for a green vinyl kitchen table and two matching chairs to appear. A large stuffed tan dog clearly meant to represent the real thing sat by the table. A youngish woman walked in stage right and rushed toward said dog.

"Écu!" she scolded, popping the dog's nose.

Since the woman did this for no apparent reason, Saul first thought she'd said "Achoo," but realized his mistake when she further scolded the stuffed dog.

A man dressed in a business suit with a power red tie strutted in stage right. "Your blouse is undone. You did not go in to work like that, did you, Ber-Ber?"

"Of course not. What would people think?"

"Yes, what would people think."

"They would be appalled, would not they, Écu?"

The man stepped toward the stuffed dog and petted it. "Yes, appalled—and rightly so. Decorum."

"Decorum!" the woman agreed.

Having seated themselves, the two poured what was supposed to represent a hot drink, since steam or vapors from dry ice rose between them. The red velour curtain went down. End of act.

"Decorum!" the five International Spa Youths shouted. Saul jumped, having forgotten their presence. Lyra, however, hunkered as if preparing for a blow, though none came.

The director strutted onstage, in front of the red curtain. "Thus Ber-Ber and Saul deliver the play's argument. We next see the Logician." Before continuing, the director stroked his white beard as if in thought, "It is morning, and the Logician has encountered Saul before the steps to his office." The director leaned to enunciate harshly, "Saul . . . is . . . not . . . wearing . . . a tie." Involuntarily, Saul felt his bare neck as the curtain rose. Onstage, the actor Saul and this new character, the Logician, entered from opposite sides. The Logician was wearing makeup that rendered his face flour-white. As he and the actor Saul collided in slapstick mid-stage, the façade to an office building was lowered onto stage left.

"I see, sir, that you are not familiar with logical syllogisms."

"I . . . I suppose not."

"Pay attention then." The Logician struck a pedant's stance, proffering his left arm in an oratorical gesture: "There are many good men in the township of Ur." The Logician twisted, to indicate an elaboration of his argument. "If all good men of Ur wear a tie, and a man named Saul does not wear a tie . . . well?" The Logician paused to look not at the actor Saul onstage but out into the audience, which consisted of Lyra, the real Saul, and the five International Spa Youth. "Well?" he asked again, in a downright shout.

Saul's head snapped forward, having been cuffed by one of the International Spa Youth. Onstage, the Logician repeated his question, stomping his foot.

" . . . then Saul is not from Ur?" the actor Saul asked, glancing out to Saul as if seeking corroboration.

The Logician moved forward menacingly. "There are many *good* men from Ur. . . ."

"Uh, then Saul is not good?" the actor said, again looking to Saul.

The second story windows to the façade representing the actor Saul's office burst open and a troupe of suited men and women sang,

> "Decorum in the forum! Decorum in the forum!
> Good is as good does, truth floats in the blood!"

The curtain descended. After a low rumbling that vibrated down to the seats where Lyra and Saul sat, the curtain was raised back up.

The redheaded bank teller stepped onto a stage now barren

except for a huge wooden vat whose lip towered four feet above her. She bent facing the vat, as if she expected a jack-in-the-box to jump out, and she cradled her wrist in pain. "Ask not!" she shouted at last. She hesitated and licked her lips before looking stage left for a prompt. Evidently getting one, she continued, "Ask not what your township can do for you, but question what you can accomplish for . . . your . . . uh . . . er . . ." The curtain went down, with a hissed "Close enough," emitting from backstage.

More rumbling with the curtain closed. When it again rose, the vat had disappeared and the office front had reappeared. The same troupe of men and women leaned out its second-story windows, but they now were tugging a heavy clothesline hung between pulleys. On the line's bottom circuit the actor Saul dangled, struggling to keep a ridiculously long red tie from strangling him. His gargles sounded so real that Saul and Lyra leaned in their chairs.

"Decorum in the forum! Decorum in the forum!
Good is as good does, truth comes from the blood!"

These screams seemed to emanate from everywhere, not just the fake office building. Real theater in the round.

The Logician walked onstage as did a new character, a blonde woman. The Logician, seeing the stuggling Saul, hurried to place his shoulders under the dangling man and provide respite from strangulation. The woman, however, blithely curtsied and said, "My name is Daisy. I am as unto the sun god, I am as unto the lilies of the field." She then turned to the dangling actor, shaking her head to reveal a long golden braid stretching beyond her waist. She proffered her arms to plead: "Saul, Saul! Cut the dreadful knot, untie the tie!"

"Decorum in the forum! Decorum in the forum!
Good is as good does, truth will float in the blood!"

A policeman with a rhinoceros's horn—or was it two horns?—appeared. "Seize the witch! Cut her strings!" the workers in the office windows shouted. The actress named Daisy started to run, but the policeman tackled her in a most unsettling and realistic manner, sending a thud through the auditorium. He then dug his horn or horns into her cleft to nudge her, on her back, across the stage in a mimic rape. Meanwhile, four actors with "Cable News" stitched in white on red t-shirts began pushing the odd wooden vat back to center stage. It evidently weighed a good deal and seemed to emit liquid sloshing. Clearly, moving it had made all the noise before. A fifth worker wheeled a flight of steps onstage and adjoined them to the vat. The policeman delivered a last blow directly into Daisy's privates with his horn, and Daisy gagged in a manner that exceeded acting. Both Saul and Lyra started from their seats; both were immediately cuffed down. Daisy's dress was ripped away by the policeman, who yanked her to her feet by her long braid.

"Aha!" the office workers shouted.

Daisy stood naked, her back to the Lyra and Saul. The five Cable News workers leered and made obscene gestures. The Logician and the actor Saul twisted to make room as she was pushed very near them. When they moved, the office workers in the windows dumped two pots of hot coffee on her, raising welts that were clearly real. When her screams died and she slumped in a faint, the Logician spoke, holding up a pedant's finger:

"Camaraderie is typically reinforced by initiatory group actions. Those who participate in group actions are good. Those who do not . . . ?"

Two of the red-shirted Cable News crew dragged the slumped Daisy by the hair to the edge of the stage, a waft of burnt coffee escorting them. A large welt covering her back appeared to be blistering already. An odd stripe of white, unburnt flesh must have been preserved by her long braid. The two twisted her about. Saul and Lyra inhaled deeply, for six guitar strings ran from Daisy's clavicle to her pubis. One of the Cable News crew slapped his fingers across the strings to send a cacaphony topped by Daisy's scream. The director, who'd slipped onstage, was now dressed in a black judicial robe, complete with a British wig that matched his snowy beard. He unrolled a yellowed scroll:

"Do you, Daisy Everywoman, denounce Isolation Karma?"

Here, an actress—the bank teller—appeared in the office's front door holding large wire cutters. She strutted to whack them against Daisy's chest, while the Cable News workers shouted, "Decorum!" The director repeated his question:

"Do you, Daisy Everywoman, denounce Isolation Karma?"

With a whimper, Daisy began playing her guitar strings. Oddly, she plucked the Rachmaninoff torch song Lyra had earlier played, "O Cease Thy Singing, Maiden Fair."

The teller angrily cut at the strings, gashing flesh, sending blood and part of a finger over three rows onto Lyra's cheek. Smelling the iron in the blood, Lyra sniffled.

"Decorum, decorum, decorum," the office workers chanted from their windows as they lit small white candles to hold to their foreheads as erstwhile horns. The onstage lighting dimmed and they walked down stairs exposed by a cutaway in the building's façade. Their footsteps were placed exactingly, as in a cow path. A rhinoceros path? The director had acquired a candle, as had the teller and all five Cable News workers. Over their shoulders, Saul and Lyra could see the five International Spa Youth holding lit white votive candles to their foreheads. The collective chanting vibrated Saul and Lyra's D strings.

Daisy had no candle. She was slumped on the floor, where blood was pooling. The director, still in his black judicial robe nodded to the Cable News workers. Setting down their candles they pulled weights toward Daisy, attaching them about her neck using the guitar strings she'd previously worn. The chanting grew. A creak emitted from the wooden vat as its sides mechanically rolled apart to reveal a Plexiglas tank of greenish water—at least a thousand gallons' worth. A turtle swam serenely in the tank, which was lit from behind. Daisy screamed, though her shout was gargled as the Cable News workers heaved her into standing.

The chanting stopped.

"*Turtur primitivus*," the director intoned.

"*Homo modernus*," the entire cast, including the International Spa Youth, replied.

Daisy was led up steps to the edge of the tank, struggling so hard that the teller had to rush and help, dropping her candle.

"The primitive turtle excels in its shell; modern man excels in its affability." This sounded from myriad overhead loudspeakers. The voice seemed familiar—one of Ur's Unitarian preachers? Once more, Saul and Lyra felt their guitar strings hum in resonance. The chant of "decorum, decorum" began so softly that neither Lyra nor Saul could place when they first heard it.

"Like unto like," the director incanted.

"Like unto like," the cast responded.

Daisy was shoved over the edge. As she sank in the green water, Saul and Lyra could see that she had not been totally stripped, that she still wore two white socks. In her struggle, one slipped off to float. The Plexiglas tank resounded with her kicks. Twice . . . three . . . four times, a metal weight vibrated against the tank's side. Then it was over. Daisy hung feet-up in the green water, her head tugged downward by the weights. After a moment, the turtle emerged from its shell and surfaced.

Saul felt Lyra's nails dig into his right arm. The theater swelled with darkness except for the tank and the many candles. From all directions lit candles converged upon Lyra and Saul. Rustling polyester filled the auditorium.

"Do you, Saul and Lyra, forsake Isolation Karma?" a voice whispered.

A pale hand thrust red wire cutters in front of Saul. He noticed bruises on the wrist.

"Do you forsake Isolation Karma?" the voice shouted, impatient.

Lyra grabbed the cutters. Saul could hear each string shiver as it was cut. One slashed his right eye.

"I do," Lyra said.

Saul looked at Daisy, still floating in the tank. Lyra nudged his wrist with the cutters. He took them and cut.

"I do," Saul said.

"Then by the power vested in me, I pronounce you, Paul and

Laura, full members of the township of Ur."

They were handed votive candles. Attracted by motion onstage, they noticed a turtle in the tank nipping at something white. What it was, they weren't certain. The warmth of the candle on their foreheads assured them it was nothing bad, nothing bad.

Ontological Reification

1.

"Excuse me!" Rosalind's voice pitched high, for a tall, dark-eyed man had just lifted her suitcase from the airport's luggage carousel and walked off.

"Stop!" she yelled. The man kept walking, but another handsome man who could have passed for his twin nudged Rosalind's elbow and said,

"Is this what you're looking for?"

She turned to his eyes, the black/brown that most African-Americans and Middle Easterners have; then she looked at the blue suitcase he pressed upon her. "Yes-no . . . I . . ." She gave a glance over her shoulder, but the other man had disappeared into the crowd, so she lifted the suitcase's ID tag, and sure enough her name was on it. But her name had been on the other one, hadn't it? Along with the purple ribbon she used for quick identification. Well, this one had a purple ribbon too.

"Yes, thank you," the man urged oddly, bowing as if he were an oriental anxious to please.

"Yes, thank you," Rosalind echoed, fingering the ribbon and staring at handwriting that seemed to be hers. When she looked up, this second man had melted into the crowd also. Lexington's Bluegrass Field wasn't that big—not melt-into-the-crowd big. Or was it? She looked around: *Sylvie's*. Was that a new souvenir boutique? And the lounge, had it always had four TVs and two bartenders?

She gave the suitcase a jiggle to hear the comforting clink of an ashtray as it bumped a bronze trivet. The ashtray was for her mother, the trivet for her roommate, who was an amateur gourmet chef. Again, Rosalind studied the handwritten, swirling, girlish "R" of her first name on the tag. An honest mistake. Jiggling the bag again she pondered just how much of her life would have drifted off had some tall, dark, and handsome took this one and left her with nothing. Her tiny Panda, which she took everywhere, which she'd gotten from her father at the age of six as a bribe for entering kindergarten. Her diary for the year. Her favorite pair of scarlet underwear that she always took on business trips just in case Mr. Special showed up in some swank hotel bar. Her blue and gold scarf, which she'd been given for Christmas by the guy she'd had a fruitless, though steamy affair with at the university. What and where was he—she cut that thought off.

Rosalind rolled her eyes on passing a muscle boy standing by a Pizza Hut. This Pizza Hut, was it new? She shook her head as the boy pushed his fist under his left biceps to make it appear larger. *Mr. Special you're not, buster*, she thought. *Talk about wearing your . . . penis on your shirtsleeve.*

As she walked outside, heat slipped up her dress, stopped by the flimsy barrier of her panties. She flagged a cab. When a dark-eyed cabbie emerged to reach for her suitcase she had to force herself to allow him to put it in the trunk, whose lid he slammed shut. *Let my life breathe!* she wanted to protest. But the cabbie'd already trotted to the driver's side and was getting in, so she blinked at the heat from the pavement and opened the back door to hop in, immediately repulsed by cushioning that had collected entirely too much cigarette smoke and spilt booze—to list its civilized stains. The *uncivilized?* Too much sperm and horse hockey from . . . Keeneland. How could she even momentarily blank on the name of that track, just outside her hometown of twenty-nine years? She glared at the driver's thin shoulders, as if he were responsible for her memory lapse.

"You—" She wanted to snip, *could have at least opened the door,* but his dark eyes bounding from the rear view mirror choked her. The cab lurched and she was thrown against the rear seat.

"Hey!" She yanked her door shut, but those dark eyes focused on the road where another cab momentarily cut into the lane. Both cabs swerved. Wrapping her arms around her torso, Rosalind noticed an ivory card protruding from a side pocket of her attaché case. Huffing, she pulled it out, giving it a twist that oddly refracted incoming sunlight:

> *Use Pencil only. This is no joke.*
>
> 1. *What was the identifying logo of the Beatles' record company?*
>
> 2. *Which Beatle was assassinated?*
>
> 3. *In what state was a gay killed and strung up on barbed wire like a ground hog?*
>
> 4. *How many humans are born every ten minutes, on this planet?*
>
> 5. *How many humans die every ten minutes, on this planet?*
>
> 6. *Who masterminded the destruction of the World Trade Center Twin Towers?*
>
> 7. *How did Juliet kill herself?*

She herself had concocted plenty of inane surveys at the computer peripherals company where she worked, but this was the damnedest mish-mash she'd ever seen. Pray tell, on just what *other* planet would humans die or be born? She flipped the card over, wondering if it represented a Mormon tract. My father has many mansions, omne pa om, et. cet., et. cet. But other than a clichéd pep talk about mind over matter, there was nothing indicating a sponsor. Compelled by the survey's pure idiocy plus a need to forget the cabby's erratic driving that seemed to have worsened outside the parking lot, she searched her purse for a pencil and soon completed all but 4, 5, and 7, with a bonus hole punched in the card from the lousy driving. She turned the card over to read,

If you have answered all seven, congratulations. The mind is a lovely gift: continue to treat it well. Water it, fertilize it, aerate and prune it—like a delicate flower. Enclose this card in the attached postage-paid envelope and return to attention of "Reification Unit."

Rosalind frowned at the phrase "a delicate flower." She hadn't answered all seven, but her roommate Heloise the Computer would conquer the remaining three. Searching the attaché's pocket for the promised postage-paid envelope she did a double take as the cab skidded. She glared into the rear view mirror, but the driver only shrugged, pointing at a pre-teen kid picking up a basketball near the bumper. The kid leisurely bounced the ball while re-crossing the street, then ran toward a makeshift goal beside a low brick house where other kids were waiting. Rosalind recognized the neighborhood from its maddening brickness.

"We're almost there," she said to the driver, surprised at the time they'd made. *Thank God*, she thought.

"Yes, thank you," he replied, bowing his head formally.

She looked in the mirror to see that this one really was oriental. She hadn't noticed his race because she'd been so intent on his dark eyes. He was probably completing a Ph.D. at Kentucky and moonlighting in this cab to buy math or computer books. If the company where she worked was any indication, they were going to take over America, and that was okay, since whining Caucasian and semi-African high school graduates seemed the best America could toss out lately. Ask the Caucasians when the American Revolution took place, they didn't know; ask the semi-Africans when the Emancipation Proclamation took place, they didn't know. And ask either about math and physics—who are you kidding?

The cab accelerated and tossed her backward again. Her palm pressed against what she hoped was stale chewing gum. Giving a hiss she concentrated on the return address that had so surprised her: Reification Unit. "Reification" was how roommate Heloise described Rosalind's job because it really wasn't in sales as such— that was taken care of at the trade fairs. Nor was it as if Rosalind had any particular expertise concerning the printers, scanners, and other peripherals her company manufactured, though she wasn't stupid about them either: she could work a demonstration and answer most compatibility questions. Occasionally she could even clear up a program conflict. Still, her main job seemed to be toting a briefcase from purchasing agent to purchasing agent along the east coast, then buying said agent lunch, dinner, or breakfast depending upon when she arrived, then leaving a slew of cute, artsy computer pads behind as mementos. "So. You're either providing an escort service, or you're into ontological reification," Heloise had pronounced at the dining room table when she moved in three months back, after the world's skinniest and tallest guy had broken up with her. She came up with the "reification" phrase on finding out that Rosalind didn't even earn commission. Of course Heloise the Computer had to explain what in Hades *ontological reification* meant.

" 'Ontology' is the study of the reality behind phenomena; 'reification' means *making over*. So. You offer a reality makeover." Thus claimed Heloise, who had majored in computers and minored in logic, having read a fair share of philosophy in conjunction with her minor. "You might even *be* a reality makeover," she'd added with a sly grin while sipping her eternal coffee. Heloise had two modes: caffeine, as in coffee black and strong; or alcohol, as in wine white and dry.

"Makeover. So. Is that like in a cosmetic makeover at Parisian's with Lancôme?" Rosalind had replied, mocking Heloise's speech pattern.

Heloise had rolled her green eyes.

"Yes, thank you."

Rosalind looked up. The oriental man was passing her a fare receipt. Nearly handing him the survey before snatching it back as if it were a hundred-dollar gift certificate to Parisian's, she passed him two twenties and waved off the change. Company money, who cared? She stuffed the survey into her attaché case and got out, not expecting the cabbie to open the door, though she'd jingled her keys in an irritated hint. Surely he'd open the trunk, though.

He did, and she was inside her townhouse at a bit past ten in the morning. She was scheduled to check in at work but called the division secretary to beg off, reading the survey as she dialed. She stared at a blank question that seemed to have grown from nowhere, like a cancer:

> 8. At *what age does the average American girl begin*
> *puberty?*

Eight? There were only seven questions before. . . . She flipped the card over: "If you have answered all eight questions . . ." She'd planned on going up to the sun deck, but her mistake convinced her that she really needed sleep. Absently letting her company's recorded phone menu ramble, she rubbed the ivory card. The survey certainly wasn't put out by the chicken plucker's union, what with the hormones infused in poultry being blamed for the alarming young age that girls were entering first menstruation. On this very trip a customer had complained that her daughter'd already begun spotting at nine, the third grade. Heloise brushed the card against her brow and punched in the secretary's extension. Maybe Mother Earth knew something was up and was trying to save humanity.

"LexMax Electronics, sales department. Hello?"

"Terri, this is Rosalind. I'm beat. Give me a sick day, anything. This was my fourth road trip in a week, and it rained the whole time until I got back."

"How about a reification day?"

"You've been talking with my roommate."

"Her joke's gotten around. The boss is actually considering changing our three personal leave days to 'Ontological Reification' days."

"Well give me one."

"You got it."

"Terri . . . when did you first begin your periods?"

"I was a late bloomer. Thirteen years, four months. Why?"

"Just this weird survey I'm filling out."

Terri warned her about cults handing out fliers to ferret personal information, and Rosalind nodded with the phone against her ear while adding nine, thirteen, and eleven—the last being the age she'd started her bleeding—then dividing by three to come up with an average of ten. She stared at her total after Terri disconnected, tapped her finger against the figures and corrected the answer to eleven. Then she called Heloise, who was supposed to meet her outside the cafeteria.

"Heloise, I'm home and I'm staying here." Rosalind had to say this twice. It was always so quiet in the section of the plant where Heloise worked. Maybe that's why she needed everything repeated over the phone, some deep-seated human need for noise. "Um, I got your card," Rosalind added.

"What card?"

"The joke survey."

"What survey?"

"Uh-huh, right, Heloise. 'Reification Unit. Water it like a delicate flower—as in Rosalind, no doubt.' So. I'll leave it by the coffee pot. You wrote it, you answer what I missed."

Once more Heloise professed ignorance over the survey, getting huffy on recognizing that Rosalind was mocking her with the "So." Actually, Heloise really wasn't the practical joker type, Rosalind reconsidered as she hung up. With a glance at the card she propped it against the sugar bowl, then walked upstairs to her bedroom, turning on a fan to get some white noise and go to sleep.

Soon she was dreaming of walking through a rock house—a castle really, except that everything was solid rock, maybe sandstone since it was shaded light tan. No, granite not sandstone, since everything looked so permanent. That permanency injected warmth onto the soles of her feet as she padded over the stone floor. One corridor slanted up, and this made her rush forward as if she would fall; the next slanted down, and this made her grunt and stiffen as if she would pull a muscle. Nothing stayed level. One room held stone furniture that grew out of the walls and floors. Under its arched doorway she found a bench, again of solid rock, again growing from the floor. She sat. As soon as that, she found herself standing, in weird non-transitional dream fashion, to look out a windowless window to see—not trees or grass, but a rock road leading to another rock house, or maybe to a different wing of this same house, since the road extended but a few dozen steps. Turning left she entered another room, one without windows, though still brightly lit as if the rock walls gave off their own illumination. Her shoulders quivered, for now the granite floor chilled her feet. But she continued on. And on. In all the different rooms she never, ever encountered another person. She did, however, smell perfume and hear a single whisper.

2.

Rosalind awoke to stare at the decorator white walls of her bedroom. The townhouse had smelled like a new car when she moved in three years ago, even though it had already had one owner, a student who'd evidently killed herself. Maybe the new car smell was part of the ploy, like baking bread to imply a cozy home in the suburbs though the previous couple had divorced. And the townhouse still smelled like a new car after three years. Did nighttime maintenance release a perfume-laden gas? Was this included in her contractual fees? In her dream about the rock house, she suddenly remembered, there weren't doors, just open archways. And there was a smell—what was it?

She heard Heloise opening the front door downstairs. *Her ratty car with its ratty muffler is probably what woke me,* Rosalind thought, knowing that the very next thing she'd hear . . . there it was! Heloise grinding coffee beans. Soon the aroma drifted up. What was the smell in her dream? She just finished dreaming it, damn it! How could she forget? She often conjectured that America was so prone to Alzheimer's not because of the aging population, but because of the intense and unnatural noise from TVs, automobiles, radios, and boom boxes. Or maybe because—

"Rosalind! You sleeping in all day or what? Get up, I came

home for lunch just so I could tell you the gossip from work!"

Rosalind heard Heloise murmur something else, probably baby-talk to the cat, so she got up and washed her face, timing matters so that the coffee would be ready when she entered the kitchen.

And it was, and Heloise was sitting in the dining room at their glass table with Sentience in her lap. Through the glass top, Rosalind saw that Heloise had bought a new pair of shoes. Daisy yellow. The woman was obsessed. The Siamese yawned widely, showing its fangs. Rosalind ignored the cat to fetch a mug of coffee. After a sip she noticed Heloise filling out the strange ivory questionnaire.

"I thought you majored in English," Heloise commented, waving the card as Rosalind sat down.

"That's my sister, remember. Psychology for me, with a history minor because of a boy I was chasing. Why?"

"Still, I can't believe you didn't get the Shakespeare quote."

"What Shakespeare quote?"

"Number Nine." Heloise read: " 'Identify the author: *Life is a tale told by an idiot, full of sound and fury, signifying nothing.*' "

"There were only . . ." Rosalind trailed off. First she'd been sure there were only seven questions when there were eight . . . well, not *sure*, with her being so tired and with that damned cab lurching about. Now there were nine. She frowned. "Heloise, come on. Did you print two of those cards?"

"I didn't print *one*. And if I had, I'd've made the questions a lot more sensible and a whole lot tougher. Ugh, who wants to think about that poor kid hanging on barbed wire in Montana? Much less Osama bin Laden."

It was true. If Heloise had stooped to a practical joke, it would have been a real brain teaser, not simpleton questions about the Beatles and obvious recent news. "Well," Rosalind asked, "did you fill them all in, the ones that I couldn't get?"

Nodding, Heloise passed the card to Rosalind. "Really? That many?" Rosalind exclaimed, referring to the answer to question four: 18,000 people born—on this planet—every ten minutes. And pulling in right behind were 6,000 deaths in that same period.

"Or that few," Heloise said. "Think how many sperm are wasted, squiggling and swimming about all alone."

"Ugh. You think about them. I haven't slept with a man for eight weeks. And he was a physical and emotional disaster, if you remember. Not only a yeast infection but he stole a dozen of our CDs.—Aha! You did miss a question, two questions." This new total of eleven questions, Rosalind decided, was okay, for if she'd missed one on the ride over, why not miss more? Heloise, however, became incredulous:

"I didn't miss anything! Nine questions. Here, let me see."

Sentience jumped onto the table and batted the card just as Rosalind passed it. They bonked heads picking the card up, and stared at one another with one closed eye each in a mirror image of pain.

"You're right," Heloise said.

Rosalind shrugged as if to indicate "Of course."

"Question ten: 'What was Moses' favorite food?' Question eleven: 'Where was the Grand Ol' Opry located?'"

"A real cultural slumgullion."

Their doorbell rang and Heloise jumped, rubbing the card as if the ink might change color. "You know those coffee mugs that have things disappear or appear with alternating heat and cool? Maybe this card's like that."

"Maybe it's some kind of shape-shifting cult thing and one of them's ringing our doorbell even now. At least, that's what our secretary warned me." Rosalind rolled her eyes and walked to answer the door.

"Nashville and Manna!" Heloise called out from the table.

"It could be Nashville, and milk and honey, couldn't it?" Rosalind shouted back. "As in the land of milk and honey, where the Lord almost led Moses?" She glanced to see that her reply left Heloise's pencil poised mid-air. Grinning, Rosalind turned to the door's peephole, to be startled so much that her knees gave. It was the Oriental cab driver.

Ever since September 11—she closed her eyes and knew she was lying to herself, for it was ever since . . . ever since . . . she'd been nervous of foreigners. Jews used Uzi's, Middle Easterners used airplanes, Orientals used . . . Sarin gas, wasn't it? Everyone was jealous of America, land of eternal youth, eternal freedom, and eternal singles bars. Through the peephole she saw the cab driver juggling her forest green purse like a yo-yo, while pointing to it and bowing politely. How the hell'd she get in without her purse and keys? She opened the door, remembering jiggling her keys at the driver.

"Purse, nice raidy," the oriental said, giving another bow.

Rosalind hesitated. Had the purse always had three thin straps? She heard chords from a guitar and glanced to her left. Their neighbor, a guy in his late forties, was sitting yoga-style on the sterile strip of lawn the townhouses all shared, playing his guitar. He usually twanged bluegrass. This sounded oriental.

"Ah, 'Sakura,' the oriental said, smiling and bowing to the neighbor, even though—Jonathon, that was his name—even though Jonathon wasn't looking their way. The oriental turned back to Rosalind: "Song about cherry blossom and spling time."

Spling time? Ah, *spring time,* Rosalind thought, picking up the cabby's phrasing, as if she were a parrot without a will of her own. She took the purse. *Thank him, you should thank him.* But he was already halfway to his cab, and its two-way radio was squelching.

So, Rosalind thought in Heloise-style, feeling more like a parrot than ever.

3.

Rosalind heard cooing near her ear and felt Heloise peeking out at Jonathon.

"Oooh, let's invite him over for barbecue. He looks lonely." Heloise said.

This was okay with Rosalind, though she had no romantic interests in the man. She was surprised he didn't own a Harley-

Davidson or a red Corvette. As in mid-life-crisis scarlet. Heloise was taking the break-up with Too-tall harder than she let on, Rosalind figured, watching her dance out onto the lawn toward the old guy folded like a yogi. Heloise wriggled her rump at Rosalind and gave her a hi-sign. "So," Rosalind said to herself, going back to refill her coffee.

After Heloise finished her lunch sandwich and headed back to work, Rosalind did go to the sun deck to read a Stephen King novel the rest of the afternoon, dozing every thirty or so pages, then waking to read more. The third doze, she once more dreamed that she was walking through the same granite house. A vague breeze, varying a note or so in pitch, wheezed its corridors like on a mountaintop. She reached a large room, likely used for entertainment, since granite benches extended from the walls and a long granite table grew from the floor. Through an open window she could see a street, steeply leading downhill. A thump, thump, like a bouncing basketball sounded. Once more, she couldn't see anyone.

The phone rang; then she heard Heloise's voice over the answering machine asking her to pick up. She reached for the extension:

" 'Lo?"

"Rosalind, that . . . questionnaire. I've been thinking about it. It's creepy. How'd you get it?"

"If it really wasn't from you, then I don't know. It was in my attaché's side pocket."

"Well, it wasn't from me and don't send it back."

"Is this what you called about?"

"Yeah, it is. They're too many creepy questions thrown in there. And how the hell's it changing, adding damned questions? Don't mess with it anymore. You don't want those people—whoever they are—knowing where you live, what you think."

"Okay Mom."

"I mean it."

"I'm reading Stephen King, Heloise. Don't keep on with the

'creepy' motif."

"Okay, sorry. Just leave it alone."

"Okay, okay."

"How about pork ribs for the cookout?"

"You sure he's not Jewish?"

"I'm sure."

Afterwards, Rosalind lay scratching her head, wondering if she'd picked up lice from a motel mattress. Lice without the carnal fun was a bummer. She created her own question, number 12: When was the last time Rosalind Rita slept with a man she cared about? But Heloise was right: certain questions you really didn't want to answer.

4.

The first thing Heloise did on arriving home—even before marinating the ribs, was to locate the survey. Rosalind intercepted her less than a foot from the trashcan, but Heloise insisted and wanted to dump it.

"Rosalind, look. It has another damned question. It has twelve damned questions!"

"Don't say it's creepy, Heloise. Maybe it's light sensitive—like lemon juice writing."

"You're right. It's not creepy. It's evil."

"Heloise! I'm the Stephen King fan. It could have . . . hell, it could have a damned time-sensitive microchip in it, it could react to skin oil. Who knows?—What's the question? Come on, what's big bad evil number twelve?" Her own recent Twelve echoed in her mind: *When was the last time Rosalind Rita slept with a man she cared about?*

Heloise looked at the card and inhaled. "All right. Here. This will prove it to you. Here. I don't want to touch it anymore."

Rosalind took the card. Sure enough, there was another question descending the blank space remaining on the card, but it was not her question Twelve. She read this one aloud:

"*12. 'At what state university were four students killed over a*

Vietnam protest?'" She shrugged and looked at Heloise, who said:

"Murder, death, you see?"

"Yeah, just like in the Bible or in a Shakespeare play or a Wonder Woman comic book. It could be worse, Heloise; it could be love, divorce.—Well? How about it? Do you know the answer?"

"No. . . . Do you?"

"Kent State. My mother said she and her boyfriend were sure the revolution had started when Kent State happened. The way she talked, I always thought maybe a hundred students were killed. But there were just four." Rosalind turned the card over. "Reification Unit," she read aloud.

"Throw it away."

"Why? It's affirming my life, realigning my misconceptions." Rosalind made a show of tucking the card in her bikini top, near her right breast. Heloise didn't laugh; she just tore open the package of pork ribs and mixed vinegar, honey, and hot sauce for a marinade.

Readjusting her top Rosalind said, "I need to get dressed, I guess, since you're the one on the make with Guitar Man, not me."

When Heloise didn't acknowledge the joke, Rosalind went upstairs to dress. Placing the card on her chest of drawers, she wasn't surprised to find another question. Why not?

13. What group kidnapped Patty Hearst, the newspaper heiress?

Another teaser from the golden oldies vault. Her mother had talked about this too, how it went along with Kent State and the collapse of society. Rosalind looked out her window, calmed by one of the few trees left around the complex. Had her mother instilled a fear of change within her? Her mother'd forsaken Roman Catholicism for two years during college, the worst two years of her life, she'd warned when Rosalind matriculated to Kentucky from high school. Breaking up with the boyfriend who was certain that the revolution was coming had returned her mother to the church's comforting structure. Rosalind always imagined the boyfriend toting a shotgun or machete on a date, but evidently his idea of revolution involved nothing more than arriving at her mom's apartment stoned and listening to Bob Dylan all night instead of making love.

A scarlet flit outside the window caught Rosalind's eye. A cardinal, then his brownish mate. She looked back at the questionnaire. Not creepy, not evil, just hi-tech maudlin. She dropped it in her garbage can and dressed in a low-cut blue blouse and hip-hugging pants just to irritate Heloise and give old Guitar Man Jonathon a double hard-on.

5.

The cookout was a success—as always, since Heloise's dad was a chef who passed his talent and his genes to his daughter. Finishing her third glass of red wine Rosalind announced,

"I'm beat. You two hold down the fort."

"She's had five road trips in one week," Heloise explained to Jonathon, who widened his eyes in fake commiseration when all he really wanted was to send Rosalind off so he could get into Heloise's panties.

"Four," Rosalind replied, holding back a yawn.

But when Heloise enumerated, Rosalind realized it really had been five. A ridiculous number, two in one day. She went upstairs, opened Stephen King and read half a page, winding up with the paperback on her nose.

Sometime later she heard a guitar playing Mozart's *Requiem.* How could anyone play that on guitar? *Why* would anyone play that on guitar? Then she heard Heloise and several other women singing the chorus, "*Dies irae, dies ira.*" Day of anger, day of wrath. She faded into sleep, into her granite house, leaning out an open bay window, still glancing down that steep, empty stone road.

She awoke again to Mozart's *Requiem.* She must have just dozed off—but when she saw the alarm clock it was three in the morning. Slipping down the steps toward the music, she stopped halfway upon seeing Heloise and Jonathon curled over one another performing sixty-nine on the couch. *God, Heloise, you do have your own bedroom.* Rosalind sat on a step to watch and listen. They were going for a marathon. Maybe old Jonathon knew some tantric yoga technique for holding off ejaculation.

Then Rosalind had to bite her lower lip not to laugh: Heloise was fumbling along the top of the couch for a piece of paper. Alongside Jonathon's weaving butt the paper looked suspiciously like the ivory questionnaire. As old J moaned, H shifted her head in the low light to read. Rosalind's eyes widened: H wrote something in with a pencil she'd pulled from an end table then replaced both the pencil and what surely was the questionnaire on the back of the couch to return whole-heartedly to more pertinent matters.

Other than an occasional shift of a leg or arm, the two resembled a natural gas derrick rocking back and forth. Rosalind glanced at her watch: about a second and a half to complete each cycle. Joining the rhythm and rocking as if in a parent's arms, Rosalind tapped her toes on the stair's green carpet. Five minutes later, H stopped her rather loud sucking to say, "Oh yes, lover, oh yes!" Compliant J worked into arpeggio, bettering the one-and-a-half-second cycle. H flipped on top, the naughty girl, her white rear squirming. It looked as if she'd maneuvered a headlock on poor J with her thighs. She climaxed twice, groaned for good measure, then started in on J. He'd already shown indications of being a male moaner, so Rosalind decided to head back upstairs. In her bedroom, she could hear J approaching orgasm, and underneath that, Mozart's *Requiem*. What a novel way to tryst.

She reached down. All that time watching and she wasn't even wet. She read twenty pages of Stephen King and fell asleep. A nearly full moon, with a thin, bladelike cloud scudding across its face barely registered on her.

6.

After Rosalind awoke to sunlight and two squawking birds, jays now, not cardinals, she checked Heloise's bedroom, which was empty, then loudly plopped one foot after the other down the stairs. Halfway down she slowed, just in case H & J were going for the Triple Crown. But the couch was empty; its Naugahyde gave off a strange metallic blue glow in morning's ambience. In the kitchen, a note by the coffee machine: *I'm over at Jonathon's playing his guitar. Guitar* underlined. *Clever*, Rosalind thought, looking for the espresso roast she saved for ridiculously sleepy occasions. Something ivory fluttered from the cupboard. Hitting her hip against the counter to catch it, Rosalind knew exactly what it was. The damned card had six more questions. Skipping the four Heloise had evidently answered between her innumerable climaxes, Rosalind read,

18. *Who said, "God doesn't play with dice"?*

Instead of the logical follow-up, "Who said, 'Don't tell God how to run the universe'?" which she knew because an upstart egghead co-worker named Francis Cox brought both quotes up every time something went wrong, there was

19. *What was Mother Teresa's favorite color?*

Rosalind threw the card in the trash and started the espresso to drip American style in the Mr. Coffee. Caffeine heresy, speaking of Mother Teresa. Walking outside she picked up the newspaper, having heard it thunk against the front door. Two townhouses away, their sixteen-year-old paperboy was peddling like a racehorse let out of a stall. He had a pair of legs resembling Arnold Schwartzenegger's—from all that entrepreneurial pumping? Rosalind lifted her arm to wave, vaguely considered seducing the kid, bicycle and all. Flesh tone, that was Mother Teresa's favorite color. No doubt it was the devil's favorite, too. Dropping her arm she stepped back inside, then told herself,

Carry your espresso and cream out back and open your privacy fence's door so you can stare at the pool and the small forest behind the townhouses. The privacy fence was another addition caused by the former owner of her townhouse, for the girl had evidently shot a peeping tom jock in the foot. Rosalind figured she would have thought of better things to do with a nice muscular college boy.

The espresso burned her lip, but she drank it anyway, feeling sweat bead from the summer morning. In the woods she spotted a shimmery patch of blue, the color of Heloise's blouse last night. A vision of her roommate's body lying dismembered with a guitar string garroting her neck jolted Rosalind and she blurted a nervous laugh. Nonetheless she walked to the pool's edge, until she saw for sure that the blue was a large piece of cardboard. *Wait a minute, I wore blue, Heloise wore yellow.*

20. Who said that the mind is a nest of vipers?

"I give. Who?" Rosalind asked of a stray leaf floating the swimming pool, expecting no answer and getting none. She scooped up the leaf and placed it poolside to desiccate. Since it was too early for swimmers or sunbathers, she sat in a lounge chair to read an article about a bookstore owner and his wife who discovered a joined pair of 40 thousand dollar stamps in one of their books. A photo showed them holding the stamps between their cuddling noses. God, the girl was a waif and the guy was at least fifteen years older. The article said they planned to sell the stamps and market a line of offbeat love poetry with the money. Offbeat love poetry?

Cherry blossom, O cherry
blossom
In splingtime I press thy petals
in my hand
While petting my lover's fleshy
botsom
And biking through a park so
grand.

Obviously no sense in submitting her linguistically racist efforts to the couple. But maybe it was time to find a job other than reification. Opening a bookstore would be neat. But other than Heloise and herself, who read, since Oprah let American literacy down after building it up? But maybe Oprah figured American literacy performed its own letdown, after that snotty author voiced his disparaging gems about her show. Who remembered *his* name? So no bookstore. What about an antique shop? She calculated what she'd saved over the last five years. About 15 grand. Enough to open an antique shop? Would she sell maudlin 60's and 70's memorabilia? If she sold baseball cards would men come in? Yeah, potbellied ones. What about a guitar shop? She stood and stuck her toe in the water. Much too cold.

21. What's the name of the classical piece used in the original movie Dracula?

"Something by Tchaikowski." Rosalind looked around, embarrassed that she'd spoken aloud. She sat back on the lounge chair and closed her eyes against the morning sun. I don't remember what I wore last night, do I even remember my name? . . . Rosalind. Followed by something alliterative because my mother loved Rod McKuen's poetry. Rosalind Rod? Rosalind Rita. Rosalind Rita Urban.

22. What pope was responsible for the Crusades?

One good thing about being raised Catholic: lots of saints to provide factoidal directions. Throat sore? Pray to Saint Blaise. Starting a woodshop? Pray to Saint Joseph. Career as a concert pianist? Pray to Saint Cecilia. Opening a bookstore? Pray to Saint Libris. Having a kinky, fruitless, philosophical, castrato email affair? Pray to Abelard and Heloise. Were they saints or sinners? Rosalind opened her eyes and saw glinting pool water. Heloise —her roommate, not the Roman Catholic waif—had told her about a guy she'd had a crush on, how he'd only responded after she started dating Too-tall, his response being passionate emails that she mostly erased. Last week when Rosalind suggested Heloise look the guy up, she'd twisted her body into a grimace like she'd been stung. So. Rosalind realized she herself could think of only one old boyfriend she'd ever want to see again, but then she heard he'd turned gung-ho and managed to get himself sent to Afghanistan. So. The blue cardboard shuffled. A rat or mouse ran out, only to disappear, evaporate, vaporize. 9-11 for the entire animal kingdom.

Today is Saturday. I can go to a movie. I can go to the mall. I can go to the library. I can walk in the park. In two hours when sunlight warms the water I can swim. I am free. Rosalind shifted in the lounge chair. She was single, but she didn't feel free, she felt adrift. She'd always imagined her soul as a butterfly and her sins as Rorschach blots, besmudging its wings. Just like her mother, she'd quit the church, to her mother's dismay. I *am* free, damn it. My soul doesn't have some indelible Roman Catholic stamp imprinted by an old-fashioned offset press. It doesn't need some damned man to open it with a key. I can go buy a small dog to chase Sentience. I can go read Stephen King. I can go back to sleep and dream. I can go visit a horse farm. Me, all by myself.

Taking a last look at the lucky bookstore couple boinking their noses, Rosalind skimmed the news: murder here, murder there. Mid-east bombings. Congressional investigation.

23. What book of the Bible says there's nothing new under the
    sun?

She remembered an English teacher at the university she'd had a crush on. He was always bringing up that book, *Ecclesiastes*.

"Boo!"

Rosalind jumped at feeling cold hands on her shoulders.

"Guitar lesson over already?" she asked, turning to Heloise.

But it wasn't Heloise. It was the doofus who'd kept half the women in the townhouses from coming out to the pool, Mr. Snag Tooth, who owned and operated an accompanying snagged mind.

"I'd appreciate your not putting your hands on me like that."

"Just a joke. What're you reading?"

"The newspaper. Do you want the sports section?"

"Thanks." He reached for the proffered section and pulled up a lounge chair, staring at her legs. She regretted wearing shorts.

After enduring ten minutes of questions about her weekend plans and the weather and whether she was going to watch the Belmont Stakes next week, Rosalind rubbed her forehead and said it was getting too hot to sit outside.

Once she made it inside she watched the doofus waddling back to his townhouse, leaving his privacy gate open, no doubt to stalk the next woman who dared the pool. The damned pool water would evaporate from loneliness if he kept this up for the summer.

24. *State the Pythagorean theorem.*

"Damn it!" She'd had a vision of kissing the doofus, her teeth interlocking with his.

At ten o'clock, after finishing the laundry and reading more Stephen King, Rosalind called her mother, who lived in Georgetown. Her mother wanted her to come home for the weekend, if she didn't have any plans. A veiled threat and insult rolled into one. Her mother wanted her to have plans, to get married and have children before she turned thirty next year and could only birth "retarded kids." "It's a clock inside every woman," her mother was fond of adding right after her political incorrectness about retardation. Rosalind waffled about coming home and asked about her father, to be informed that he was in the garden. She imagined being married to the poolside doofus, him on his knees planting carrots, and nearly laughed aloud. Instead:

"Hey Mom, what do you suppose Mother Teresa's favorite color was?"

"Is this a joke?"

"I . . . no, I'm just curious."

"Well, Princess Di's favorite color was baby blue. Don't you think Mother Teresa's would have been the same?"

7.

Rosalind put on a baby blue blouse, blue jeans, and white cowgirl boots that she hadn't worn in over a year. Last Fourth of July, in fact. She sat at the kitchen table, reading Stephen King. At 11:20, Heloise walked in.

"Get his guitar tuned?"

Heloise grinned. "Had to restring it."

"My, my."

"I've been thinking about that questionnaire. . . ."

Rosalind glanced to the garbage. Was Heloise going to flip

sides and claim that the questionnaire came from a supreme supernatural being? If so, she'd flipped her wig as well as her side.

> 25. *What was the name of the young nun who taught Rosalind Rita Urban in the seventh grade only to be retired to a mental institution six months later?*

> **Sister Mary Thomas Red Face**: What we still have to explore, children, is how essence manifests itself in substances such as the soul. Now, girls and boys, God is pure essence, the Prime Mover. Everything else has to be moved by something—so humans aren't really even essence, but only form locked inside matter, like music inside a violin, which must be plucked for music to take on essence. Music means love. Music means touching one another.

Rosalind heard a cough and realized that Heloise was talking, somehow mixing philosophy and the questionnaire. That explained Sister Mary Red Face. "Stop it, Sist—stop it Heloise! Stop! Let's go to the mall!"

"Stop what? I'm just giving you the bottom line. That questionnaire is reifying our joint psyche. Between us we've answered all the questions. The ones you answered reminded you of your mother, and the ones I answered—"

"Last night?" Rosalind prodded. Heloise blushed.

"Yes, last night. They reminded me of an old boyfriend."

"Could he play *guitar*—" Rosalind sang the word—"as well as Jonathon?"

"Jonathon's no slouch."

Rosalind bit her lip to stop a porno rhyme: *No slouch, no slouch, even on a bright blue couch.* As Heloise blushed Rosalind envisioned Sister Mary Thomas's pimply face surrounded by a virginal wimple, like an Indian beset by a smallpox-contaminated blanket.

"We—you need to go to Victoria's Secret for some sexy

underwear to corral Jonathon." Again, Sister Mary Thomas's pimply face intruded—what was with Heloise and this blushing? Sister Mary had simply disappeared in the middle of the school year. Was Heloise going to disappear?

After agreeing to go to the mall, Heloise changed clothes while Rosalind started coffee. Heloise came down in a slinky yellow tank top. "Let's go," she said, pouring coffee, then stooping for the kitchen garbage. Rosalind, realizing that the questionnaire lay on top, stopped her. Couldn't Heloise see it? They shouldn't toss it just yet. Should they?

"The bag's only half full; save a tree," Rosalind offered, not willing to admit her true concern.

Heloise shrugged and left the can alone. Stepping outside the front door, they waved at Jonathon, who was once more on the grass playing his guitar.

" 'Sakura,' " Rosalind commented.

"What?"

"That's what he's playing. It's a Japanese tune about cherry blossoms in spring time."

"Wow. I must have really rocked him last night," Heloise said, slurping coffee.

8.

When they entered the mall, Heloise pointed to a yogurt stand. "I always want ice cream after sex."

"Yogurt's not ice cream."

"You know what I mean."

Rosalind rolled her eyes as Heloise ordered vanilla yogurt with M&Ms and cashews.

26. What nut was Washington Carver famous for?

Rosalind placed her right hand on her left and pinched hard. This obsession with questions was worse than the week she walked around staring at men's crotches and imagining taking their warm penises in her mouth, their hot jism clinging to her tonsils like Elmer's Glue. To turn her mind she began to count the number of people wearing black—male and female. And when they walked into Victoria's Secrets she counted shades of rose panties and bras, pushing Heloise, already in a willing mood after twelve hours of guitar strumming, to buy a dozen rainbow sets, to the fandango tune of $288.76.

"This obliterates my budget," Heloise commented as they left the store.

"I'll buy your S & Ms—your M & Ms—until our next paycheck. I'll even carry your Victoria's Secret shopping bag for you, just in case any of your repressed friends from the computer programming division are lurking in the mall."

Heloise stuck her tongue out; nonetheless, she passed the distinctive pink striped shopping bag to Rosalind upon spotting a tall blonde guy in the music store. "He's a friend of Jonathon's. They jam together."

27. On what farm was the first hippie music festival held?

"At least he's not old enough for Woodstock." How come her mother didn't have any neat memories like Woodstock about the hippie days? Music, burnt bras, and patchouli incense?

"Lay off, Rosalind, Jonathon's not that old."

"You'd better check his driver's license."

"I already have. He's forty-four. He wouldn't have even been born when Woodstock took place."

Rosalind didn't bother to correct the miscalculation.

Just before they reached the music store, a dark-eyed man intercepted them. "You dropped this," he said to Rosalind, enunciating each word as if practicing English. *And, nice madam, can you tell me donde est la biblioteca et las terroristas?* He kept his right hand behind his back and offered Rosalind his left. At first she thought he was handing her the ontological reification questionnaire. She snatched it before Heloise could get a look, but it was only Heloise's receipt from Victoria's Secret. When Rosalind smiled, the man brought his left hand forward to give her rose-colored panties. He pointed to a hole in the shopping bag. Rosalind looked from his dark eyes to the receipt, where she could swear that she read,

    28. In what year was Kentucky accepted into statehood?

It was her turn to blush, though she managed to thank the man. When he walked off, she turned to Heloise,

"Do you know what I thought he was handing me?"

"The questionnaire?"

Rosalind nodded.

"Who is Ted Bundy?" Heloise asked.

"What?"

"That's one of the questions, or it should be. 'Who is Ted Bundy?'"

"Question 29?" Rosalind half said, half asked.

"Let's go meet Jonathon's friend."

The closer they got as he played guitar, the handsomer he became. He wasn't as old as Jonathon, and he could play guitar at least as well, but in a soothing nylon string manner as opposed to the twangy bluegrass Jonathon typically played—"Sakura," being a total exception.

"Chris? Hi," Heloise said.

He looked up, continuing to play, then registered Heloise's face and smiled with clean, even teeth that signaled some dentist's financial delight. His cheeks flushed just enough to make him interesting. Cute as a tall button, Rosalind thought.

"Jonathon said the two of you are playing at Linden's tonight." Linden's was an espresso/wine bar.

"That's right. We start at seven." That dental smile again.

"Oh, Chris, sorry! This is my roommate, Heloise."

Rosalind laughed. "You're Heloise, Heloise. I'm Rosalind." Another guy was walking over, a salesman, maybe. Before she lost her chance, Rosalind blurted out, "Do you know what year Kentucky was accepted into the Union?"

"1792."

Rosalind impulsively touched Chris's hand in thanks. It was smooth and warm.

"No problem," he replied. With his smile, Momma had taught

him well. They tentatively made plans to see Jonathon and Chris.

The salesman was going there too, it turned out. He had dark eyes that gave Rosalind the creeps, so they left Chris and went back into the mall.

"My sister Haley says that one out of every three spouses in America met their spouse in a mall," Heloise commented, stretching to watch another guy, this one dressed in shorts and wearing a muscular pair of legs.

"In a mall, huh?" Rosalind spotted a gargoyle atop some store marquis and bowed, offering a mock prayer. "O Great Presence of the Mall, give me succor."

"I don't doubt her, you know. The next great American novel will be entirely set in a mall. Maybe with an interlude where a dark-eyed middle easterner wheels a cart around, pretending to sweep but spreading Anthrax. And did you mean sucker with a k or succor with two c's?"

"Both. Wouldn't the guy wheeling the anthrax around die too?" Heloise asked.

"He wouldn't care. He'd be swept—no pun intended—into Paradise where virgins would wait on him."

"That lets the two of us out. No succor and no sucker."

"Praise Allah." It had taken Rosalind a moment to realize she wasn't a virgin. Surely it hadn't been that long that she'd slept with a man. For it to regenerate, that is.

9.

They wound up crossing the parking lot and entering Joseph-Beth's huge bookstore, since Rosalind decided that what she needed to cheer her up was something literary and sad:

T. Anne Vise
Author of *Sybil, Too*
will be signing her book today

Someone at work had told Rosalind about the book. It was

another *Sybil*, another multiple personality book, though they now called it DID, Disinterred Identity Disorder. "Disassociative Identity Disorder," Rosalind corrected herself aloud.

The author, T. Ann Vise, appeared to be borderline midget, and her makeup glowed garishly, as if she'd just finished filming a science fiction movie. Rosalind and Heloise approached the line, which had over a dozen people in it, since *Sybil* reportedly took place at the University of Kentucky's Medical Center and that name was having a butterfly effect regardless of this book's quality.

> 29. *Freud, in his later writings, posited this drive as an*
> *addition to the sex drive. What is its name?*

No one ever figured out why the girl who'd owned the townhouse had killed herself. Her note only said, "I'm sorry, everyone." Rumor had it that her autopsy showed her pregnant.

When Heloise stepped aside, Rosalind smiled and held her own book out for signing.

> 30. *Jung, contradicting Freud, said that every part of a dream*
> *reflects . . . not wish-fulfillment but what?*

> 31. *How many states are in the Union?*

> 32. *What country gave America the statue of Liberty after its*
> *own bloody revolution and after America's own bloody Civil War?*

> 33. *Does love really mean never having to say, "I'm sorry"?*

As Rosalind leaned forward, T. Anne Vise looked up with a smile that quick-froze—a shrimp packed for market. T. Anne's therapist had been glancing at another customer, so it took a moment for her to realize that something had gone awry. When she did, she yanked two autographed books from beneath the table and handed one to Rosalind and one to the last woman in line. T. Anne's chest was heaving. Rosalind couldn't take her eyes off its violent motion.

"I . . . I . . . I . . . ," T. Anne stuttered.

"We have to leave." T. Anne's therapist knitted her brows at Rosalind and put up a sign that claimed the author would return in half an hour.

"Can we help?" Heloise asked, since the therapist was trying to lift the woman from the chair.

"No. Just leave. That's best."

"I had a dream . . . about a granite house, with granite walls and granite furniture and no people—"

"GO!" the woman shouted, tugging at T. Anne. A staff person from Joseph-Beth glanced at Rosalind and tugged at her green vest as if loosening a canister of pepper gas from its Velcro.

10.

"Who founded IBM? What is the name of the last stallion that won the Triple Crown? What's the difference between Tennessee Sour Mash and Kentucky bourbon? Bill Monroe is the founder of what type of music? Jesus is the founder of what religion? How many chucks can a woodchuck chuck if a woodchuck could chuck wood?"

"Rosalind?"

"Rosalind?"

"Rosalind!"

The car smelled of carbon monoxide. *But I'm not committing suicide.* The exhaust system made noise. Sixteen chugs per minute, sixteen humps, like an oil derrick. Sixteen traffic lights. Happy, happy birthday, baby. Sweet sixteen. Though you're not really my baby. *Who was Rosalind Rita Urban's boyfriend when she was sixteen in a muggy Ohio Valley summer? With whom did Rosalind Rita Urban climb a fence to sneak into Fourth of July Fireworks at the University of Kentucky? If you could name six people important to your life, in alphabetical order, who would they be?*

"Rosalind!"

They were standing before the townhouse. Rosalind thought she saw Jonathon, but it was only his fancy guitar stool. Or maybe an indentation in the grass. Jonathon was getting ready to go to an espresso and wine bar and play guitar. Every Good Boy Deserves Favor. What about every good girl?

"Rosalind!"

"I need to find the Ontological Reification survey."

"Fine. Let's go inside."

For some reason, Rosalind thought they were at the river. Bobby Allman's. Or getting a martini made from moonshine at Allman's competitor's place. How come Allman's always burned down every four years? Symbolic of its name, All Men? Was it like that bird that rose from its ashes? What was the name of the restaurant across from Allman's? The one that didn't burn down. Hunt's? Horace's? Hall's? But they weren't at the river, she hadn't been drinking.

"How many trips did I make this week, Heloise?"

"Five. You made five trips, Rosalind."

"I need to find the Ontological Reification Survey."

"We all need to."

They found Heloise's younger sister, Haley, sitting on the blue couch, reading her eternal poetry and drinking overcooked coffee. She snuffed her menthol cigarette before Rosalind could say anything.

"Hi." She wasn't even sticking to the jism love left on the couch from the night before, for she miraculously peeled free from its blue to stand and hold out her arm to support Rosalind. "What's—"

Heloise brushed by to lead Rosalind into the kitchen. Rosalind tugged the garbage can from under the sink, but a virginal white plastic bag lifted breezily, instead of a bag full of the past and holding the precious survey. She fell to her knees.

"Where—"

"I thought I'd do you two a favor and take it out."

Rosalind twisted to go outside, but Haley said, "The garbage truck came an hour ago. I watched it empty the Dumpster over its head, I mean its cab. Was an earring or something in there?"

11.

"Who first ate the apple in the Garden of Eden?" Rosalind asked, turning from Heloise's sister, who was dutifully holding a ballpoint pen.

"Who built the Eiffel Tower?" Heloise countered.

"What city is the home of Motown music?"

"Why did Moses have to take off his shoes?"

"What year did Daniel Boone leave Kentucky to go to the Alamo?"

"How many Beatles were there?"

"What psychologist wrote the book *Beyond Freedom and Dignity*?"

"Who conceived the Big Bang Theory of the universe?"

"In what state can homosexuals legally enter into a marriage?"

As instructed, Haley was writing down each question, then each answer, once Rosalind and Heloise agreed that they'd gotten it right. But whenever Rosalind leaned to confirm what Heloise's sister was writing, she feared that somehow . . . somehow they'd never get the ontology right. Because wasn't reification remaking? Wasn't remaking undoing? Wasn't undoing undone? Somehow, some way, they'd always slip and get the ontology wrong.

The Tree of Knowledge

It was chilly and cloudy, heavy clouds that might threaten snow if this were not by the Gulf of Mexico. Well under these clouds Evelyn Couchet passed a bakery and was deluged by an urge for two cream horns, specifically two cream horns with a honey and black walnut glaze. She pressed her nose against the bakery's window, careless of what phlegmy panhandler might recently have done the same, for this urge was a livid thirst stretching up past her esophagus to parch her tongue's taste buds. Can one thirst for cream horns? Evidently so. Feeling wind blow off the building she edged closer to the window.

When she'd been pregnant two years before she'd craved frozen strawberries and fresh plums until twenty-four hours before miscarrying. Why not cream horns now, in her sterility? Evelyn had to balance herself against the plate glass, for despite the chill wind, a sick heat passed through her lungs. Recovering, she walked inside.

But the bakery carried only beignets, chocolate chip cookies, and funnel cakes.

"The chocolate chips're great," a pimply girl behind the glass counter suggested. "Gooey."

"Do you have them with black walnuts?"

The girl stared at Evelyn, who closed her eyes on hearing the store's front door open. Along with a customer, a waft floated from the street. Was . . . was that the smell of cream horns? No, for Evelyn heard the girl addressing the new customer, a male who stank of cigars. Evelyn opened her eyes and walked out.

Left or right? Like her brother's bird dog, she thrust her nose into the air. It was late morning, so the stench of Clorox and vomit had dissipated. The Big Easy. Why call it that, when nothing comes easy? Not even cream horns. After ten meandering, sniffing blocks, Evelyn wondered, Was my namesake Eve this obsessed with the apple? And, Why do they call it the Tree of Knowledge when it led her only to trouble? A patrol car slowed on seeing Evelyn testing the air with widespread, canine nostrils. But the cop either recognized her from her shop or had more pressing matters, for he drove on. Go right, she decided, not because the aroma was stronger in that direction, but because right led to the river.

Owning a figurine shop in the French Quarter, Evelyn felt obliged to wear high heels. Today, their patent yellow leather drove through her tibia, femur, pelvis, and vertebrae until their sidewalk clack shattered her teeth's enamel to remind her that she didn't cradle even one soft, gooey cream horn in her mouth, much less two.

Why two, she questioned, avoiding a UPS man she didn't recognize as he rushed to deliver packages, twisting his hips with the shifting weight of the packages. Ah, just like he balanced two packages, the satisfaction of two cream horns balanced with bicameral authority: justice for the first pastry; wisdom for the second. She giggled as if a young girl and turned onto another street. Another. As she wandered, she wondered, The pelvis is such a very large bone . . . how can the clack of tiny heels not possibly be supported and cushioned there?

Was the smell of honey and black walnuts stronger? For that is what she finally realized she must be smelling, the glazing on the pastry, not the pastry itself, not the cream-filling inside. She stopped, watching another UPS man struggle with a shop door. Funny, she didn't recognize this one, either. Just how many parcels could be delivered in the French Quarter? How many needs fulfilled? How many UPS men employed?

Over there, across the street . . . Gustave's Coffee House. That was new, wasn't it? Evelyn shifted between a parked car and scooter, looked both ways, then ran across as fast as her yellow high heels would allow. Cream, horn. Horn, cream. The words crisscrossed until she laughed at the sexual implication. Horny creamy cream-cream. She shook her head angrily. One damned need at a time was enough. "Sufficient is the evil unto the day" rang in her head as she hopped up the curb. She supposed that oddball quote came from parochial school. It sounded like a nun thing.

She stopped short at the entranceway even though she was sure she smelled black walnuts—if one can smell black walnuts. She stopped because every customer inside Gustave's hunched over a tiny, oddly triangular table to peer down at a demitasse or a china plate. From her vantage, it appeared as if each table were stabbing each customer's belly or sternum with a triangular point. There were at least a dozen solitary diners—no, more than that, for the restaurant opened deceptively inside. The nearest woman surely was a tourist, for she simply wouldn't believe the weather might be cold in New Orleans on her vacation. Her thin black shawl and shimmery blue dress indicated as much. She quivered sculpted pearl fingernails over . . . Evelyn nearly lurched, for two cream horns reposed on the woman's plate, swaddled in a linen napkin. The woman looked up, eyes darting. She covered her pastries, sensing Evelyn's intent to grab and run.

"Don't."

Evelyn turned, but there was no one.

"Do."

She twisted, but the tourist remained mutely intent on her pastries, nor did any maitre d' lean in French Quarter nouveau mannequin fashion to coax Evelyn—or anyone—inside. So the combative voices must have been Big Easy echoes, like hushed praying in the cathedral, like flesh roasting in the various sarcophagi. They say that two months and it's over in one of the family vaults, given a good hot summer—baked until only a bone or so remains. The femur, maybe. I walk, therefore I am. An enameled tooth, maybe. I chew, therefore I am. I hunger, therefore I am. I need, therefore I am. I hobble, therefore I am. I don't have, therefore I am. But in a burial vault, what need or want could be left?

With a melodramatic grimace, the tourist stuffed the first cream horn in her mouth, deep-throating the damned thing to belie her crocheted black shawl. Nearby customers followed suit, gulping drinks and cramming food into their gullets. Evelyn rushed toward the counter. Once there, she couldn't believe the empty showcase. Dainty doilies galore, with grease spots galore, but absolutely nothing on display, though each doily had a price card.

A dark-faced man appeared. He could be Cajun or Turkish. "Yes-s?"

"I—"

The man's hands leaped to a doily that held two cream horns. From where? Two-forty-five, the card read. He didn't even bother with gloves or sterile wax paper, but plucked the pastries with his bare fingers. In the back of Evelyn's mind she angrily thought about phoning the health department, but the front of her mind was a kaleidoscope sparkling "**Cream Horn.**"

"Five dollars and twenty-one cents, with tax."

Evelyn felt her humerus, radia, and ulna shaking unto her clavicle. She snapped open a small yellow purse and spotted: her driver's license, a Platinum American Express card, a breath mint, keys to her shop, and a five-dollar bill. She plucked out the bill.

"And twenty-one cents."

"I . . . I just left my shop for a walk. I work three blocks over on Royal. Evelyn's Figurines? Evelyn, that's me."

The man shrugged, his facial creases outlined darkly with the gesture.

Turkish, Evelyn decided. You goddamned foreign son-of-a-bitch. She thought about grabbing the pastries, but the man pulled them out of her reach, though still managing a salesmanly smile.

Someone was pressing behind, Evelyn could hear and smell the breathing—ragged and foul, as if too much coffee and too many cigarettes bred an eternally dry mouth with sulfurous odors. Evelyn extracted her Platinum American Express card, her fingers clasping it like forceps. Before any part of the card was visible, the man behind the counter curled his lips contemptuously and tapped a Magic-Markered sign: Cash only. Following that were phrases in at least a hundred languages, presumably conveying the same message, though food residue covered an inch-wide oval where the languages became obscure. Not just the Health Department, but IRS and Immigration. I'm going to turn this sonofabitch in to anyone who'll listen.

"Uh, lady, do you mind?"

Evelyn twisted toward the reeking breath. "Look, do you have a quarter? I need a quarter to buy these pastries."

The man sneered, glancing at her legs and yellow high heels. Evelyn felt her lips pucker seductively, felt her knees wobble, and her fingers tremble as if she might kneel, unzip the jerk and give him a quick blow job in the middle of the shop just to get his quarter. But her friend Tomi Sue stood in the front door.

"Tomi Sue!"

Evelyn had to call her name three times before Tomi Sue noticed her. Tomi Sue gave her a quarter and Evelyn paid the Turk, telling him to keep the change. Then she searched for a table she and Tomi Sue could share, but all the tables were the triangular single-seaters. What kind of idiot restaurant was this? She scooted a chair forward and leaned over the two cream horns. The table's triangular tip bit her chest like a knife. Her finger quivered upon touching the sticky honey. If she ate this one, there'd only be one left, and they were small. And the one she ate would be gone. She could feel saliva welling in a tidal flood. Her shoulders rose with a happy thought: What if I eat just half? But then there'd only be one and a half left. What about just a nibble, say half of a half of a half?

She eyed a piece of black walnut glistening with honey. She could pluck it, smell it, mince it with her incisors. She'd hardly notice it was gone, and there'd still be two cream horns remaining.

Her fingers acted. But the piece of black walnut fell. In a panic she leaned, but the piece had become lost in the floor's wood grain, like some mummy under tons of sand. It remained lost, no matter how hard she peered, and though she kept her left hand in contact with the two cream horns, she began to fear someone would nab them, so she sat upright.

From a table behind, she could smell the man with the bad breath. The sonofabitch from Turkey or Aglakistan or Hades had deserted the counter. Evelyn looked for Tomi Sue. Nowhere. She glanced at her wristwatch: twenty till one. She'd been away from the shop nearly two hours. How? She gulped the two cream horns and ran out, banging a table, knocking a customer's plate on the floor. A mournful, baying howl arose, but she had no time to apologize.

In her shop, two notes had been slipped through the mail slot: one was from a customer obsessed with military figurines who'd drop three grand in a blink. His handwriting was shaky. *Be back at two. Please be here.* The second note was from Tomi Sue. *I'm sorry,* was all it said, other than the signature. Sorry? Why?

Evelyn placed the notes and the mail on her desk and dusted the shop to keep busy. A second craving for cream horns and black walnuts overcame her as she picked up a Chinese mud figurine—a trio of wise men, from their looks, one walking, two seated, one of these extending his hand—to offer a seat to the walking figure? Were they gathering for a lecture on the metaphysics of time, the genesis of the world? Evelyn realized that she couldn't remember eating the cream horns. She fought an urge to call the coffee house, overcoming it only when she realized she couldn't remember its name. She eyed the clock: four minutes after one. Fifty-six minutes until the customer for the military figures would return. She dusted where the mud trio had resided. Before replacing them she noticed something in their eyes—a longing for a bluer sky, a fresher stream, or a different lecture.

2.

Eyes haunted Evelyn for the rest of the week. Tourists' eyes, customers' eyes, street people's eyes, shopkeepers' eyes, dogs' eyes, the figurines' eyes—just what distant field were they focusing on? If all they were camera lens, she decided, they'd be searching infinity. Even the old guy with his tin soldiers. His eyes had been rheumy when he'd come back, as if the lead in the tin soldiers were finally poisoning his system. He'd licked his fingers as he'd written a check for twenty-two hundred and sixty-eight dollars for a set of Napoleon's and Wellington's troops at Waterloo. Evelyn imagined him carrying the set home and licking his fingers as he placed each one in a showcase, as if dropping them back *in utero*.

It was Tuesday of a new week. She'd been open two hours, and spotted the same note from Tomi Sue. *I'm sorry.* Evelyn still couldn't fathom why. She gave Tomi Sue a call and asked if they could meet for supper.

"Meat?" Tomi Sue asked this so abstractly that Evelyn filled in the inappropriate spelling, thinking of dazed cattle being churned into hamburger. When she imagined a teetering brindled calf, its eyes were focusing not on her but somewhere else, even as the sledgehammer descended—or the drill or whatever unpleasantry they used these days.

"Meet, yes." Evelyn's throat caught, for she'd been about to suggest the place with the cream horns before remembering its odd seating arrangements. "At Acme's."

"Mmm, oysters and beer." But Tomi Sue's "mmm" carried a whole battalion fewer m's than it normally did, say the entirety of Napoleon's and three quarters of Wellington's army gone missing in action or AWOL.

They met at Acme's directly after closing their shops. Tomi Sue and her girlfriend owned a high-toned art gallery, but as Tomi Sue gallantly pointed out, who didn't, in the French Quarter. Tomi Sue loved to slum, which was why Evelyn had been surprised at the abbreviated "mmm."

"What are you giving up for Lent?"

Evelyn's throat tightened. She eyed the beers two nearby couples were drinking, but all four mugs transformed into upright cream horns.

"Cr—" Evelyn felt eternally grateful that a waiter approached before she had to commit. Lent was two months away, anyhow. When the waiter left, Tomi Sue was holding her face in her hands.

"Something wrong, Tomi Sue? You and Rita getting along?"

"I'm sorry," Tomi Sue said. Those two words carried the same shagginess evident in her note. "It's not Rita, it's not the business, it's . . ." When Tomi Sue looked up, Evelyn choked. How could her friend have aged five, six years since the coffee house? A scar Evelyn had never noticed squatted on Tomi Sue's chin. Nearly an inch long, it resembled the "pocket cuts" Evelyn still carried from her hysterectomy.

"You never answered my question. What are you giving up for Lent?"

"Cream—" But the final word caught in her mouth. If she gave up cream horns, what would be left? Evelyn started to correct herself and say "Sex," but that was a sad joke these days. Two minus one equaled zero. Nouveau math for Nouvelle Orleans.

"Cream horns? Wasn't that what you were ordering in Gustave's?"

Evelyn nodded. The waiter brought their drinks and they toasted.

"To the good life!"

Oddly, Tomi Sue withdrew her glass. "Skol," she offered instead.

"Skull," Evelyn agreed, clinking her wine glass against Tomi Sue's mug. "Why'd you write 'I'm sorry' on the note you left in my door last week?"

Tomi Sue looked briefly into Evelyn's eyes, then away. "Because now you know."

"Know what?"

"I could tell by the way you asked for the quarter in that coffee house. And I heard you bum the guy behind you for one. So now you know that it's never going to end, that even if you sell six hundred figurines during Mardi Gras, even if you give up cream horns for Lent, it will only be something else. It had to occur to you sometime in your life. We've all been amazed that you've held out so long, especially after . . ."

Tomi Sue was a tall, handsome woman, with a bent toward histrionics. A drama major, she still performed in local theaters when time allowed. So her words and gestures, including the ellipsis, carried to the table with the two couples. But instead of rolling their eyes or bending their ears for local gossip, Evelyn saw them grasp their loved one's digits, as if assuring themselves of youthful, mobile phalanges. So what Tomi Sue said had touched a chord with them, along the lines of Mozart's *Requiem*. Evelyn's face fell, as if a puppeteer had sliced a guy wire or supporting muscle. She realized that she wanted, more than anything, more than sitting with her friend Tomi Sue, more than the vintage Cabernet before her, certainly more than the forthcoming oysters or watching couples holding hands—she wanted two cream horns with black walnuts. That would be . . . Edenic. Her stomach churned as she deliberated a polite way to leave. Gustave's would be open until ten.

"It's all right," Tomi Sue said. She extended her left arm just as the mud figurine back in the shop had, as if indicating that the lecture was about to begin. Or maybe that it was over, and that was all there was to it. Evelyn realized that Tomi Sue's "It's all right" strode the air as disconnectedly as her previous note's "I'm sorry" had.

Tomi Sue stopped at two-dozen oysters and two beers. Evelyn drank three glasses of wine. Hardly the bacchanal one would expect just two blocks from Bourbon Street.

Little light remained when Evelyn walked toward Gustave's Coffee House. She felt herself pulled by the thought of two cream horns. How was it, she wondered, that she wasn't gaining weight? In fact, her clothes were beginning to hang. She imagined a life of cream horns. There would never be enough. Two by two, she'd pluck them from the tree and eat them, yet an empty plate would always remain, a full bough would always hang just a bit higher. She'd always want more. Would she have wanted more and more babies? If she had given birth to the little girl, would she have wanted a boy, twins, triplets? If Paul had stayed, would she have wanted another husband, an illicit lover, a pet sex slave? Did Eve want more and more apples? Bushels? Carloads?

Gustave or whoever had already twice raised the price of cream horns, so she was carrying a twenty. She'd even considered pinning a hundred dollar bill to her bra. Tonight, once again, the price had gone up—honeybees were to blame this time. They were supposedly dying across North America, some deadly fungus eradicating them. Cream horns were now $7.95 apiece. Evelyn sighed in relief. She'd have enough, even with tax.

"Could I have a glass of water with these?"

The Hades creep leaned back for Perrier. "Three dollah extra."

Great. Now he sounded like a parody of the three mud figurines. Immigration was going to have a trip with this idiot. Time, little Amehlican missy, it exist ever and ever to change. When desire get what it want, when empty cream horn turn to full, then full—so solly—drain to empty, like big Buddha's belly-burp joke. You undahstand, yes?

"Never mind. I'll take them à la carte."

3.

Her shop had always comforted her like a hut. From Scandinavian trolls to axe-wielding Chinese warriors, every inhabitant had been a friendly lodger. But somehow all the figurines now faced the register, and Evelyn studied not their grins or their body language, but their eyes. It was a mistake looking at the eyes. She'd watched Tomi Sue in a play called No Exit where eyes created hell for everyone. It was a mistake in that play to look into someone's eyes, it was a mistake in the French Quarter, it was a mistake in her shop.

She considered torching the shop. She envisioned carrying in a cheap yellow and red can of gasoline, hearing its thin tin musically bonk as she emptied it. But her upstairs apartment would go, too. And all her neighbors. She couldn't jeopardize them. She imagined their staring, accusing eyes: the middle-aged gay couple, John and Tommy; the New Orleans spinster and her aging Doberman; the new couple from Atlanta who mysteriously made scads of money working at home. And they kept parrots. Parrots live over a century. Eyes staring for over a hundred years, wanting cream horns or birdseed. What did all the fat Buddhas in her shop want? More rice? More humans to laugh at in mock empathy? The Napoleonic soldiers, what had they wanted? More blood, more booty, more women to rape? The little Swiss girls— did they want more cuckoo clocks or more Swiss boys? Wasn't the Buddha supposed to be thin? Her entire shop was filled with wants. How much more so out on the street?

Evelyn did take to pinning a hundred dollar bill to her bra after the price increased because of the honeybees. Two cream horns now cost over twenty dollars. She sent a friend in, thinking that sonofabitching Gustave was jerking her around. The friend reported that they didn't have cream horns, but that the chocolate éclair that she'd bought cost nearly ten dollars. "It's inflation. The Secretary of the Treasury needs to investigate New Orleans." Evelyn stared into her friend's hazel eyes, which were focused on the wall. When Evelyn turned, she saw only a stark white-and-black clock, its numerals all cutely jumbled in a pile at the bottom where six normally resided, with a sign reading, "Who cares?" The bloody, racing second hand gave the lie to that. Everyone, that's who. And when she turned from the speeding red second hand, her friend's hazel eyes were already backing out the door, signalling apologies that they had to be somewhere.

It was then that Evelyn understood. Yes, little Missy, you will always care, though for what, you will never be sure; you'll always want to be somewhere else, distracted into acquiring two cream horns. And those around you will also always want to be somewhere else, acquiring whatever they think they need, cream horns or strawberries or chocolate-covered cherries.

She started for the river.

There was always a crew of panhandlers along the river. Evelyn recognized them through the seasons. It was now a month before Mardi Gras, however, so new ones had begun to pop up. If she were a man, she'd answer the bait "I bet you ten bucks I can tell you where you got your shoes. . . . On Bourbon Street, ha-ha!" with "No, I've got them up your stupid ass!" And give a demonstration . . . to boot—ha-ha! But a number of the panhandlers were desperate, so that wouldn't be wise, even for a guy.

Evelyn leaned against the railing and looked down into the Mississippi River. A dead fish had washed up, and its cottony, swollen belly made it look as if it weighed twenty pounds or more. She thought of fairy tales involving rings and babies and gold coins in the bellies of fish. Before she could talk herself out of it, she clambered over the railing, landing with an unpleasant crunch that snapped a high heel and made her think she might have broken or at least sprained an ankle. A tarsal?

Stupid. How was she going to open the damned fish's belly, anyway? She leaned against the sea wall, pressing it to her scapulae. The river smelled, the dead fish smelled worse. Water was lapping. If she waited, the tide would come in and she'd be carried away. The wall was warm, since the winter cold fronts had moved out, flowing back up north to haunt the Plains states and the Canadians. Her tarsal wasn't broken, since she could move it. She watched it momentarily circle, as if rotated by a magnet, say in sympathy with the earth or the tides or some approaching black hole.

What if she opened the fish and found two cream horns inside? Her giggle dissipated into the lapping water. Two soggy cream horns would be about right. She leaned toward the fish; its exposed eye was filmy, silvery, gray. Never to see again. And though the fish's mouth gaped, it wasn't moving, was it? Even with all that water around them, fish still always swim, wanting more. Well, this one didn't want any more water or shrimp or worms or coral or whatever it had eaten when it was alive. Any more cream horns. Wanting over, little fishy. Time gone big belly up.

Evelyn realized that her blouse had ripped in the jump. She felt for her scars and imagined them puffing in the warm water, swelling. No, that wouldn't do. She looked left, then right. About a hundred yards away she caught sight of rubble she could climb, and she limped toward it.

When she pulled herself out, she looked directly into the panhandler's eyes. He must have heard the noise and gotten curious, thinking maybe a whale or a magical mermaid was emerging from the river. He didn't show surprise when Evelyn put on her broken heel and stood unevenly on the pavement. The safety lights glowed, but the two of them, Evelyn and the panhandler, shifted in their own world of wants, far from anyone else.

"Bet you ten bucks I can tell you where you got that yella shoe, lady."

"Ten? Why not a hundred?"

He was skinny but tall, and still wore a heavy coat despite the warming weather. He looked at her, then around. "Okay, bet you a hunderd.—You got 'em on the sea wall in New Orleans. Give me my hunderd." He swaggered and licked his lips.

Evelyn tugged at her bra and handed him a nice, almost dry hundred-dollar bill.

"Damn!" He turned and held the bill to the light, then half-trotted off.

Evelyn counted his steps. Two, three, four . . . they slowed and he looked left and right . . . five, six. He stopped mid-stride of his seventh step, stuck the bill in his pocket and walked back. One wouldn't be enough for him, she knew. One wouldn't be enough for anyone alive.

"Bet I can tell . . ." he started. Then he just glared. "Give me more," he demanded hoarsely. He put his right hand in his pants pocket and bunched it into a fist that bulged.

"I don't have any more."

"Give me that yella little purse there. You got more."

"No I don't. Even if I did, it wouldn't satisfy you, would it?"

"What the hell's that suppose' to mean?" He drew out his

fist and unfolded a knife in a smooth motion she wouldn't have believed him capable of. "Do it, bitch. Give me more or I'll slice your damned lily white throat."

He was white himself, so why focus on that, Evelyn oddly thought. She smiled, as if the puppeteer had finally restored her guy wire. Maybe it wasn't a smile, maybe it was a gasp for the air floating around. Would her mouth be open tomorrow when they found her? She envisioned her blood draining, momentarily quenching some passing roach's or fireant's thirst, draining and shrinking the scars on her stomach until she could walk any beach, draining and shrinking her stomach until she could pass any pastry shop in the Quarter without ever bothering to sniff the air.

"Little mister, you don't have the guts," she said, dangling her purse over the sea wall, twisting it enticingly under the safety light. He lunged and she grinned; she knew they both did.

The Great Humus

Marie: I still imagine her full brown hair between my fingers, still smell its autumnal life. But without its true, fibrous and soft touch, I've languished for weeks. The trees . . . they too languish. I can tell by how they sing, as I look from my window onto their lamenting outlines battering the dark. Because of Marie I languish for weeks, they for centuries.

—What? Yes, I understand: you trees have rooted unhappily much, much longer than mere centuries. How human of me.

The twin pin oaks outside my window were the ones who just now chided me with that notion.

—What? Yes, yes, all right then, just now *sang* to me. "*Sing, sang, say, chide*, what's the dif?" I mutter when it seems they aren't listening. The desk I sit at—its wood looks so like Marie's eyes. Her eyes . . . did I say? Her eyes were brown and full of autumnal life. Of a sudden, a pointy leaf ticks ghoulishly against my screen, a displaced Poesque heart.

I pound the autumnal brown desktop: "All right, all right, so you sing! All right, all right, fa-so-la, so you've been unhappy much, much, longer than mere centuries!"

Pardon me.

Imagine feeling the earth turn. Trees can do that, you know, for bereft of departure or any other motion (besides an occasional sway plus that inexorable upward growth), they live to send their tongues into the earth's mid-section much as we humans send ours to explore a lover. So trees caress and tickle the earth, who in turn gives suckle. But you shouldn't think of trees as mere fragile appendages to this great humus. No, they're bulk, their trunks, thickness upon thickness, press in a most comforting, immovable, undeparting manner. Imagine that density's assurance!

. . . Hearing a tick, I lean, bulging the screen outward with my nose and brow. Viewed from my window, the neighborhood trees form a chorale, it too ever thickening, elevating the great humus over any human's petty rafters. . . .

Yet trees have lightness, spirit. Of course they have, so they might vocabulate with dirt—agh! A troublesome prickling ticking pin oak leaf outside my window intrudes again with its grating scratch—All right all right, then: *sing* with the dirt. Is that what you want me to say?

Marie. . . .

Still, its and other leaves outside continue to bristle. *Call you the Great Humus dirt?* they screech inharmoniously in archaic diction, like some Bible story of forsworn, wailing love. *Prideful beast! 'Tis not a cheap carpet woven for your soleful pleasure.*

All this, I sense, touches what angers them: For some time, eons or even aeons, they've watched us humans shilly-shally in bundles of electric hurry, our spindly feet never standing still (*Never! Never!* quoth the trees) to respect the earth, feel its flux.

Never, never, say I. Marie's coffee cup remains on my desk. Do her lip prints still reside? I reach, ask, say, see, sob. . . . Never, never.

So! the trees sing. *It was eons past when we came to consider ourselves earth's ambassadors, eons past when we gathered in enclaves, what you humans call forests, wherever the earth directed us. Oh yes, the earth sings magnificent directions—though you dirty mortals never wait to stop to stay to abide to rest in its majesty. Instead, you're always departing, always talking.*

"Earth moves its magnificent bowels, we fritter our tiny vowels," I joke. But trees have no humor. Tapping the wood of my desk, I counter their sullen silence: "So-la-mi-do. So mutual misunderstanding's the problem, isn't that it, guys and gals?" (Some male and female ginkgoes rootfully reside down the block; I'm sure they must be able to hear this conversation.)

I await an answer. I should explain that the trees are telling (singing! singing!) me all this through a mixture of song and image. It's like primitive, vulgarized MTV, though I don't let on that I think so.

TV, they sing, catching my thoughts regardless. *Stupid words atop stupid words. When you furless bipeds first appeared—so-mi-la-la—you could communicate more clearly than now. When you first appeared we trees understood your every grunt through its tone and sustenance. There were no insinuations, imputations, or connotations as in your so-called modern speech. What was, was. Some—*

"Let me guess," I interrupt. "The great vowel shift changed all that."

So-so-la-do, the trees sing, once again ignoring my joke. *Some wondrous evolution you've undergone now, some sartorial sophistication! You humans were musical then. In fact, music was the basis of humanity's language then. Successive high notes meant excitement, alternating low notes meant happiness. Yes, la-la-ti-ti, alternating*, the trees insist, singing to spite my crinkled brow. *In that era, happiness had little to do with monotone possessing. Possessing is the droning hobgoblin of your modern life. True happiness embraces flowing, alternating.*

"Departing?" I scream. "Does it embrace departing?" No I don't. That is, I don't scream. I sigh. The trees are right: we haven't evolved, but devolved. Being human at that wondrous inception must have been like being a rocky brook, a windy mountain pass, a hawk hovering a thermal, two squirrels mating and chattering among branches. As I think this, my heart swells in timpani.

Do-do-re-re. There were a series of low gurgles for human rutting, the trees intone. *Which is all*, one ginkgo chants, *that makes any sense about you humans now.*

I push my nose angrily into the screen. The ginkgoes are too far away, but the pin oaks could have spied in my window and gossiped throughout the neighborhood about my nights and days with Marie. After all, the green couch we made love on is visible over my shoulder in another room. "Did you do that?" I shout, swatting at the red leaf on my screen. "Did you spy on us?"

There was one couple, la-ti-la-do, that our olden tree ancestors were particularly fond of in those days of yore.

"Olden? Yore? You ninnies! Did you?" I cruelly bang my oak desk as if to punish an imprisoned kinsman of theirs for their woodsy impudence, their romantic sylvan withdrawal. Marie's coffee cup almost lands on the floor, but I catch it on my foot, panting, relieved to see that it hasn't broken, for it is the only thing she left, besides, besides, me.

With this man and woman, fa-so-la-do, we came to regard humans as something other than mobile bumps. We came to see you as a higher life form. This man and this woman, though a trifle underdeveloped, seemed proof of humanity's potential.

"Because they were a simple couple," I guess, resuming my seat at the desk. "Back-to-nature. Primeval hippies sans PC's, chain saws, or automobiles. Peaceful. Loving." My throat catches on that last word.

The trees titter, as if I'd finally told a joke they could understand. If so, it's one I don't understand. Though I'm talking only to the trees outside my window, I feel trees worldwide titter instantly. I hear and see leaves rustle over the Pentagon, over nearby Fort Knox, over a burned-out tank in Iraq. Fronds clatter before evil, drug-filled Miami alleys as Sabal Palms take up the word "peaceful" like a sizzle stick might tickle a cymbal. *Peacefulpeacefulpeacefulpeaceful. Such a word*, the trees laugh musically. *Like all your words: only words. Like LOVE. Loveduploveduploveduplovedup*—this oaken bass crashes at me, counter-pointing the sizzling cymbal.

I'm sullen and rap my fingers on the desk, thinking revenge.

Do-do-fa-mi, the trees sing, in a whirligig of angry merriment. *Peacefulpeace-fulpeaceful*. Visions of flopping speared fish, brain-dazed cattle on wobbly knees, and headless chicken carcasses tread-milling blood-spattered legs—all these attack me. Then—most abhorrent to the trees I suppose—uprooted vegetables lying limply, suffering passively. *Peacefulpeacefulpeaceful* melds into a gruesome, off-key Gregorian chant.

"So . . . the couple weren't peaceful," I guess.

Trees don't have shoulders, so they can't shrug. I push my fingernail angrily into my long-suffering desk. My fingernail bends like a discarded love-letter. A wisp skitters my neurons and axons: *Not peaceful, but in love.*

"Not peaceful, but in love," I repeat to the trees. I expect a reply, yet the trees remain incommunicado. The visions are gone, as is their song. Slowly, I realize that it's left for me to sing-think the heavy-browed Cro-Magnon couple. . . . Ah, there they stand in a drooling lurk before their apartment. Apartment? Before their cave. Does the male look familiar? I rub my inconsequential chin, and he shivers then tilts his head like a Valentine bear plashing out puppy-dog blinks toward his mate, whose tangled brown hair tickles her breasts, whose eyes form two moons large enough to tame any saber-tooth tiger prowling the earth.

"Look, look; see, see, you trees! That's love, or a small part of it."

The trees remain rooted and silent; not even termite groping emerges. I hastily recite Hallmark Card sentiments and hum some Andy Williams and Julio Iglesias to further convey my meaning. The trees don't shrug, no; but something resembling their previous bass sounds out: *loveduploveduplovedup.*

Of course. What we've come to call love is little more than possessing, frantic clasping. Our clutching love must seem ridiculous to stately trees. Could they ever clasp? Form the two-backed beast? Root limbs, riffle leaves, or redden bark with passion's heat? "Hey you ginkgoes out there! What about it? I know you're male and female. I took high school botany. Do you do anything besides exchange DNA by wind currents?" In answer, a frantic wallowing accompanies a prolonged pant. The resultant high C illumines my mind with a sad, incandescent blue, like a three a.m. wail haunting the backside of a funeral parlor. *Dearly departed, we are departed here today to . . .*

"Get off it, you trees! Sex isn't all that bad. In fact, it's damned good!"

What's that tugging? Is my oak desk stocking my feet as if I'm a wayward Puritan? *Marie!* My toes squeal in crescendo, ten *castrato* Placido Domingos.

So-do-do-re, such a bore, booms a basso voice. This voice doesn't belong to any tree in the neighborhood. Its deepness offers a fatherly hum. The walnut by the highway? I wait, but the voice only repeats its phrasing, *lente e undignificado.*

I think of Marie, but cannot fine-tune her body, her face. I can only hear her feet, her lovely feet—were her feet lovely? No, they were chubby and boyish, but, still, why did they depart?—I can hear them walking across my kitchen floor and closing my kitchen door. Tip-tap, tip-clack, for ev . . . er.

I again sing-think the Cro-Magnon couple, with maybe some Las Vegas crooner in the background. Immediately, trees outside my window counter by projecting images of men blanketing women, women blanketing men, panting, panting, like wide-eyed animals dashing before an exploding forest fire, their tongues swollen and extended, their legs taut, their fingers clutching.

"So the couple weren't particularly in love," I offer. "Just what then, so impressed your ancestors, O Worthy Trees?"

So-la-la-la. I'm given an image of a man planting seed—not, I hastily add, in the venereal, but in the agrarian sense. This planting evidently astounded the trees, for while they could drop their own berries acorns and fruits, they hardly possessed skill or compassion enough to plant other species' seeds, nor even cultivate their own. I watch the Cro-Magnon digging his stick into the ground lovingly, in a most caressing manner almost as if he were . . . I think of Marie in her loving stage, not her leaving stage. I think of unhooking her bra to let it freefall across her spine's furrow. I try to remember the exact shade and shape of her nipples and aureoles, but the image fades, so I look out my window to the trees. "Help me. You were watching, after all," I plead. "Tell me the color. Tell me the texture of her lips, describe the dance of her eyes."

Wordsdirgewordsdirgewordsdirge, rattles in cowbell madness as a Norwegian pine jolts back a lurid image of the primal couple coupling. I grab the cord to my Venetian blinds and yank them shut.

Fa-so-la-ti. You humans! The trees sing-shout this and somehow open my blinds. *Such blasphemous rebellion from the soil: hop here, hop there, hop away. So blasphemous that we once hoped you would hop from the earth, hop for a celestial twinkle,* the Norwegian Pine sings. *But we sadly gave up that hope,* the Mimosa from my neighbor's yard adds.

Do-do-re-so. For many years, all the trees sing in chorus, *we celebrated human demise and decay brought by plagues and floods. And when you yourselves invented war, our very roots curled with happiness. This is the moment, we said, when they will all hop away.*

I'm filled with images: bodies of dying mastodons, dinosaurs, and boas—and piled indiscriminately atop these are cities of human corpses, all rotting, all rejoining the Great Humus. *Hopawayawayaway.* I pale and bash my desk to avenge the gore, but it continues, continues, continues.

The symphony enters another movement:

Ti-la-so-do. Remember the man and woman? The trees sing-ask. *Of course not. Your memories are so fragile, so temporary, so departful. When the man and woman and their children first snuggled near us for shelter, we trees were content with this new ambassador who seemed to happily spread earth's good news by seeding.*

Do-do-do. The groan of that beats against my bones. *Do-do-do,* tree limbs repeat, as if I weren't frightened enough. Marie, where are you? I need you.

It was at this time, the trees sing on, *that you humans sounded utterances other than song. A stand of apple trees had congregated where the family planted seed. One day the man and woman were in the field, humming and planting as usual, when the apple trees heard the male emit a great toneless roar:*

"Mine!"

He took his stick and scraped away humus the woman had just tamped, leaving seeds exposed to the sun's heat. The woman retaliated by scraping away humus he had tamped.

"Mine!" she too shouted.

We trees were stunned. These sacred ambassadors had fouled earth with pettiness and vanity, leaving it cleft and barren. As our forebear apple trees watched, the pair forsook shouting to hit one another with sticks. Finally one stick broke and the woman lunged, leaving it in the man's stomach. He fell, she ran. We had sacrificed our branches as tools and this was the use they came to: weapons. For quite some time that day, we observed the man twitch. Ants and vultures congregated and we celebrated as of olden and even compacted to call up lightning in self-sacrifice from the earth whenever you humans sat under us for shelter.

The curse the man had used, "Mine," quickly echoed through the forest until all of you were speaking instead of singing, fighting instead of planting. This curse denied your potential. We trees decided that a grave falsity adhered to the very act of speaking, of naming and thus divorcing things their musical ties to the Humus. Attempting such eternal possession delivered a prideful and vulgar slap against earth's gift of life, a gift too precious to be anything but evanescent.

Evanescent Marie. Depart, depart.

I see heat lightning in the distance. One of the pin oaks must have spotted it too, for its lower limbs tremble and scratch my screen, anxious to be inside.

I laugh. I laugh and laugh and laugh. "You immobile lightning rods are nothing but pulp for our furniture and newspapers! We humans rule the earth and sky, we'll rule the universe someday, you dirt-bound morons, you would-be telephone poles, you sappy saps!"

I stare outside my window as lightning illumines sentinel trees in the distance. Mine. What part of that landscape is mine? With both hands I clutch my wooden window frame. A piece crumbles in dry rot. I still can't envision Marie in her lovemaking, only in her leaving mode. Tip-tap, tip-clack. What part of her belonged to me? What part of any human belongs to another? Your whole body's your mate's, celibate St. Paul admonished us. Then he rejoined the Great Humus. Did the trees rejoice at his tiny death-thump? Undoubtedly. More lightning, powerful in the distance. What part of anything belongs to humanity? "Love," I whisper. That small part. But if love departs?

Loveduploveduplovedup . . .

Marie, Marie, Marie . . .

I open eyes that I call mine, but the dark presses. Seeping in, from outside a window screen I call mine, I smell the chlorophyll bulk of a rotating earth, that great humus through which we all must churn. I smell that, and an ever-approaching night.

All Lovely, in Their Bones

1. Turn

How many people ever share a dream? This is what they almost asked one another over the email, after a computer whiz girlfriend showed them how to turn off the snooping device for their company's computer server. All the time, people went outside for smoke breaks, and she had just quit smoking while he had never smoked—so why shouldn't the two of them be allowed email breaks? Anyway, this dream-sharing that they almost had came with the first emails they exchanged. Heloise sent this one to him, feeling minuscule amperage flitting through wires:

I had the strangest dream. I was in a room—a bright enough room, with a bank of low—knee-high low!—filmy windows, though I only saw them peripherally. The floor was that old type of linoleum that came in a huge roll, and it curled in all four corners of the room. Maybe there was a mouse nibbling in one corner. So, like I said, there was light—summer sunshine—filtering into this room. Through one hazy window I caught sight of a hardscrabble field and a handful of scrub pines. What I stared at for the rest of the dream was an empty shelf. I stared at this eye-level shelf, awaiting maybe a whisper from another room, or a soft whistle to float in from outside, or the sound of footsteps. I knew that the person speaking, whistling, or walking would hand me something memorable to place on the shelf. So I stared. The shelf's wood was rough, almost as if it had been hewn with an adze centuries back. When I tiptoed, splits along the wood became visible. My right hand twitched, ready to place something on that shelf, maybe a knick-knack from a state fair. Do people still go to state fairs? I didn't think that then, but now. My heart thumped and my hand stayed tense. That was the entire dream, and it lasted all night. I thought dreams were supposed to last just 30 seconds. All night, staring at an empty shelf. What do you think?

For more than a month before this email, all of January and half of February, they had worked together on designing an in-house newsletter. When he walked into the room, she smiled. When she walked in, he smiled. Smiles like sunrise over the Grand Canyon. Sometimes when one of them asked a question about the newsletter they would lean forward in their silent seats. It was a wonder that wintertime's static didn't propel them into one another's arms. For that entire month and a half it seemed to her ordained in the stars that electricity—AC, DC, or winter's cold static—would eventually pop between them. *I've always wanted to learn to tango,* she said one day when a tango came over the radio station. *Me too,* he answered. There, see: the stars were already forming constellations. Glancing up to one of the ridiculously high windows (just the inverse of her dream), she caught sight of a daytime moon coldly smiling. Looking at his computer screen he heard molecules swirling, passing themselves off as dust motes ready to tango.

The project room they worked in was large and weird—but maybe not, considering that the computer peripherals plant covered five and a half acres. The room had been designed as a catch-all for old manuals and handbooks, but for nearly four decades employees had tossed in everything from the contents of a single woman's desk (she'd been killed in a car wreck coming to work), to discarded travel posters (Rome! Paris!), or ex-family pictures left from divorces. By the double doors sat one stack of romance books, one stack of mysteries, and two of science fiction. Occasionally, someone would drop a book off in one pile or another and quietly scavenge for a replacement. It was the plant's informal trading post. She'd cough or dig a sharp elbow into him to point out the scavenger, and he'd grunt.

On the back wall facing the doors, two windows left only the sky and treetops visible, since those windows stood so ridiculously high, seven feet from the floor. Perverted, as if a misanthropic architect had designed the room to forever tease its occupants with occasional glimpses of a dropping autumn leaf or dancing snow flurry or the hanging countenance of a cold moon. Still, the two of them had opted to move two computers, a scanner, and two printers into this huge room, reasoning that the surrounding memorabilia would inspire them in their first newsletter, which was to be a double issue reviewing the plant's history, from its inception of manufacturing electric typewriters to its present manufacturing of color printers, FAX machines, and scanners. Memorabilia aside, upon their first appraisal of the room, molecules in their bodies perhaps felt a tug of anima and animus, of kiss me and I'll kiss you, and this had also urged them to opt for the room's relative seclusion. If truth be known—if truth between two humans can ever be blueprinted into any mapped surety—they were assigned the secluded spot because their supervisor judged the in-house newsletter to be a feely-touchy waste dreamed up by a vice president with nothing on her mind.

Movement 1.) They learned right away that both of them had graduated from the University of Kentucky.

"So. Did you take a class with See-see Bones?" she asked.

"Didn't everybody? Even though I majored in philosophy I took her."

See-see Bones was the nickname students gave Professor Clarissa Circle, a physical anthropologist who peppered her lectures with a wealth of strange murder stories and even stranger personal philosophy.

"A girl in my class asked her why she ever got interested in anthropology if she really felt that human interaction was basically impossible." She handed him a dozen pictures showing Christmas party activities. They were looking for one they could label, *Bah! Humbug.* The photo they would wind up choosing—they dropped the *Bah! Humbug!* idea—was one reason their newsletter's January turned into a smash hit plant-wide.

"You're kidding. That girl had a set of cajones. What did ol' See-see answer?"

Heloise ignored the sexuality of the remark. "She said . . ." Heloise had returned across the room to her swivel chair. She placed her knees together, noticing that Abe had been glancing at her ankles and legs. "Professor See-see said, 'First, while I don't think people are stupid, I do think that they are genetically doomed to live a fantastical lie—a conundrum. The fantastical lie being that they can truly touch one another in a meaningful way. And secondly—and more importantly, young lady—I'm a physical anthropologist, not a cultural one. So all people are at least lovely in their bones.' "

"You've got her answer down pretty well," he replied. "Uh, could the girl with the cajones have been named Heloise?"

They smiled at one another in their Grand Canyon way.

Movement 2.) Heloise saw their mutual smiles as posing a challenge to Professor Circle's theory, a challenge she welcomed since she hadn't dated any man steadily in well over two years. All her one-night stands supported Professor See-See Circle's theorem in a most depressing way.

Movement 3.) One day when she was napping at her desk, arms crossed, he stared, watching her breath's rhythm, imagining her heartbeat. His wife was buxom—a Jewish earth-mother, she called herself. Heloise was thin, as he imagined Heloise of Heloise and Abelard must have been. And Heloise was feisty. Could he be her Abelard, he wondered. She awoke, shook her head upon catching him staring, and smiled. He smiled back.

Movement 4.) One day when he was stretching toward a high shelf holding some strange bit of the past that might give them a cutesy newsletter angle, she rested her head in her palm to watch. Throughout high school and college she'd dated only rail-thin guys like herself, smokers who quickly made up their minds—and just as quickly changed them. She inhaled deeply. He was chunky, and

Joe Taylor

she already knew that he thought laboriously over each detail of design, just as he laboriously and stubbornly reached to pull down what looked like an orange Donald Duck. What would chunky, laborious, and stubborn—muscular, persistent, consistent, she optimistically revised—what would that combination be like? On a date? On dates? Kissing? In bed? Twisting, he saw her staring and fell backwards into the shelving.

Though they laughed, neither of them spoke.

Movement 5.) They only began emailing when they no longer worked the entire day together, when they only saw one another in the mornings. This scheduling shift came despite the fact that their first newsletter was such a hit, for the vice president and their immediate supervisor had calculated that since the first was a double issue the two underlings could put out a monthly newsletter in half the time and still perform part of their previous jobs the rest of the time. "We're gerbils," he told her when they got the news. "Or automatons, like in the Taylor Time Study done in plants last century." Because of this schedule shift, she stepped matters up. And he had vague stirrings of some unsettling lacuna each afternoon when they were apart. She stepped matters up by sending the email about the dream to his desk in some cyber part of the plant that she didn't care to locate by foot. He thought that lacuna only indicated he missed the space of working in a big room.

You, he answered by email, *have something to take and to give. That's clear from the dream. You're like Nietzsche's Zarathustra descending the mountain because he's so overfull that he must share. Pardon me,* he then wrote [she thought this a rather stiff apology for email] *pardon me, but I was a philosophy major at Kentucky and I come up with crap like this still.*

She thought the metaphor charming. So . . . muscular, persistent, consistent, and intelligent. She drove to Joseph-Beth's that evening and found a copy of Friedrich Nietzsche's *Thus Spoke Zarathustra,* reading the first 70 pages, which followed a hermit descending from a mountain. Fitting, she thought, that this man quotes Nietzsche, who appeared to be a razzle-dazzle loner. I wonder if he keeps that huge brown walrus moustache because Nietzsche is his hero. She never told him she'd started reading Nietzsche.

Movement 6, Contra-move 6-A.) It was maybe during the fourth week that they worked together. She became bold with her body contact, thinking that chunky and laborious and hard-headed might need a push. When she stood next to him, she'd press her hip against his shoulder. When they laughed at some employee sneaking in for a science-fiction or romance book, she jostled him with her elbow. One day she wore a different perfume and sensed that he was about to reach and place his arm around her hip. Oddly, this unnerved her and she jumped away, though they continued talking about the layout for the "Memorabilia" section. Go *figure*, she thought that evening, analyzing her evasive action. On the next day, frustrated with both herself and him, she began apologizing for even the slightest contact between them.

Movement 7.) But now, weeks later, with the emailing, spring would soon be on them. "I thought I heard a robin singing outside my apartment. You should see my apartment: I've painted the walls lavender and off-orange," she said one day before lunch.

I forgot to tell you, she emailed later on that day. But she had a failure of heart here, for what she wanted to email him was, I forgot to tell you that I saw you looking at me, the same way that I look at you; I forgot to tell you that I have an antique brass bed; I forgot to tell you that I changed to blue satin sheets since I thought they'd match your eyes even though they clash with the lavender. What she emailed him was, *I forgot to tell you that we need to check the photo on page three. It needs cropping.*

The first Friday that they worked together, that is, after they'd been together only four days, he carried in a set of dumbbells. She raised an eyebrow, because he didn't seem the jock type, a little too chunky. At nine-thirty, as she walked outside to smoke—she hadn't quit cigarettes at that point—he started lifting the dumbbells. Was he making some weird health comment? Screw him if he was. This partly ruined her Friday, for she'd chosen a short blue blouse that showed her mid-riff, just to see if she could get a rise from him, even though he was married and even though plant policy frowned on such dress. This was then they were hidden away together for the whole day, and a friend had told her that his wife was Jewish and ten or so years older than him, almost forty.

Movement 8.) He surprised her after lunch one day by coming out on her second cigarette break, even though the weather was bitterly cold. She stood by a low concrete splash wall. He stood far enough from it and her that the smoke wouldn't drift his way. Inside the room they'd been talking about churches and God while looking at old photos on their cutting table. The conversation spilled to her smoke break:

"There's a church in my hometown," she said, "that's ruined the lives of two women."

"How's that?" he asked when she didn't continue.

"It's stuewpid," she said. "Just because the two women get together for lunch at one another's houses, the church women gossip that they're lesbians."

He didn't care about lesbians. What he cared about was the quaint way she turned the vowel 'u' in 'stupid' into a overgrown diphthong. She was upset, but he was concentrating on a diphthong. Then he concentrated on her eyes: they were green hazel, his favorite of all eye colors, malleable, changeable, unpredictable. He noticed that she was winding down her rant about the church because he wasn't returning the ball. *You*, some part of him surely whispered to some other part of himself, *are stuewpid. You are a dip without a thong. Listen to her; talk back; make movement.*

He had dreamed the same dream. About the empty shelf, that is. Not on the previous night when she had, but some time around, say, Valentine's Day. But that morning when he received her first email, he and his wife had argued about going to see her parents, who were retired in West Palm Beach. The last time they'd visited, he'd overheard her father saying that "every Jewish-American princess can be forgiven one goy mistake as long as she corrects it in time to raise the right type of family." What disturbed him most was that Judith had simply replied, "We'll see." So, pre-empted by arguing with his wife, he hadn't told Heloise about having the same dream, just as she hadn't told him about reading Nietzsche.

After the January newsletter they both got a raise. With her raise she bought a used piano, something she'd wanted since graduation from Kentucky as an English major and journalism minor. His raise, Judith insisted, should go into a retirement fund. "Abe, you're only twenty-five," she said. "Think what that extra hundred a month will mount to forty years from now." His wife, being seven years older than him, planned for the future constantly. Even when they made love, she'd bathe first and insert a cream for lubricant that discouraged oral sex. It was because of his name—Abe—that they'd met. She'd thought him Jewish. But he had been named after Abraham Lincoln because his mother had been a caretaker at Nancy Todd Lincoln's home in Lexington. It was the one time his wife hadn't planned for the future. Did her father's phrase "goy mistake" keep ringing in her ears because of her lapse?

Movement 9.) During the second full week they worked together, Heloise was listening to poetry on a tape player when he walked in. He stopped at the door, Monday-numb. He'd never heard anyone listen to poetry, though his wife occasionally listened to murder mysteries on tape when they drove anywhere over an hour. Teasing him, Heloise began reciting poems at odd times during the rest of day. "My mistress' eyes are nothing like the sun," she'd recite. And he'd blush at the word 'mistress,' until she continued the poem and told him it was by Shakespeare. Clean Willy.

"Oh," he said, arranging photos on the desk. Actually, he liked the poem: it was funny for a love poem: like Heloise with her quick grin that revealed abundant gums, with her equally quick ironic curling lip that people easily missed. He went home that night and found—as he suspected—that his wife had placed a green leather-bound Shakespeare in their living room bookcase, to assure visitors that they were literate. The green complemented the surrounding books, which were tan. He felt the gold leafed pages clinging like Saran Wrap. Then he found the poem Heloise had recited: "I've never seen a goddess tread; my mistress, when she goes, walks the ground." He leaned against the mantle looking through the living room's plate glass into the winter dark. It was supposed to snow: he used to walk the streets during snowstorms, day or night. Glancing to the closet that held his coat and gloves, he caught sight of Judith in their den reading a mystery and watching TV at the same time. He looked back at the poem: "my mistress, when she goes, walks the ground." Heloise had the oddest habit of popping up onto her tiptoes; he'd caught her doing this several times. Thinking she must have taken ballet, he asked; but no, cheerleading, she answered. "I can't imagine you as a cheerleader," he replied. "That's what everyone says. I can't either, now. People change." He'd blushed when she said that, though he couldn't tell why.

He didn't go walking, although the flurries were thickening outside the window. He went to Judith and rubbed her shoulder. When his reach extended to her breasts, she shrugged. He looked at the small TV, with even smaller comedians dashing off lines in a sitcom, and he said, "Let's go make whoopee." Judith pulled down the bifocals she'd recently brought and countered, "What? Why? Did you run into a gorgeous secretary at work?" He waited until she went to bed, then closed the bathroom door, and sat with one of her Victoria's Secrets catalogs. Occasionally, a hard crystal of snow would hit the window in a gust of wind.

It was on a Wednesday. One of her friends was supposed to meet her at Jackie's that night for drinks, but the friend called as soon as Heloise unlocked the double doors to say that she had a date with the guy she'd been eyeing for two weeks. Heloise congratulated her, looking out the two high windows at a blank sky. Two weeks? Heloise fumed after she got off the phone. I've been working on this guy for over two months. The night before she'd read in *Cosmopolitan* that any girl who hadn't tried S & M with her boyfriend by her eighteenth birthday was going to be a sole holdout in America. Maybe that's the ticket, she thought. After all, he's married to a woman nine years older than he is.

Movement 10.) So when they were going through photos together, she said, "I can be downright wicked when I want to be." He smiled. An hour later she said, "This little girl wants someone she can kick around." He'd been walking out the door—to the restroom, she presumed—and he turned, knocking two books off one of the stacks. The fantasy stack? "Just kidding," she said.

When he came back, she wasn't there. Out to smoke, he presumed. He noticed her purse, an unpretentious terrycloth affair with red and green striping, left on the table. This wasn't good because they worked in a relatively secluded area of the plant and who knew who might pass by and see the opportunity of an open purse. So he placed it in a chair. He liked to do that, take care of little things for her. Then he thought of what she'd said about wanting someone to kick around. He had almost blurted, "I'd be happy to volunteer," but then she'd said, "Just kidding."

When he drove home that night, he realized that he'd been thinking of Heloise while he'd stopped at the grocery for hamburger and while he'd passed the mall. And when his wife mentioned flying to see her parents, he couldn't get Heloise out of his mind.

In February, on a lark, Heloise brought a virginal white card that read, "Valentines are such special people." She felt sure it was innocuous. Still, she forgot it at her apartment, leaving it by her antique brass bed with the blue satin sheets that matched his eyes.

Movement 11.) When they'd been working together eleven weeks, he found out that he'd missed Heloise's birthday, so he bought her a book of poetry. Looking through it at the store, he chanced upon a poem that started out "I knew a woman, lovely in her bones." It fit Heloise so well that he re-read it four times. She opened the present the next day, and he insisted on reading part of that poem and was surprised that she knew it by heart, so they alternated lines. That night he felt as if he'd gone on a diet and lost twenty pounds. They spent the rest of the week working on the third newsletter, with him laboriously placing and re-placing photos and text until it was perfect.

Movement 12.) *Dear Heloise*, he emailed twelve weeks after they met, one week after the late birthday present. *Our third newsletter's almost done. I think this whole concept is doing a great deal for company morale.* He'd thought about emailing her something goofy-sexy, like how her toe rings would catch his calf hairs if they rode a tandem bike together. Or better, something true, like how he loved to watch the profile of her face and imagine the dimple in her chin. But a deadline for an advertising brochure loomed. And his Doberman needed to be spayed. And he remembered two credit card bills.

Yeah, she thought, reading his email about company morale. But she didn't answer it. They didn't even need the no-snoop back door for that one.

Her friend Cheryl had been trying to get her to date a friend. "He's a skyscraper," Cheryl said. "And thin, like you." Heloise had held off, thinking of constellations. But all last week, after the book of poetry, had remained flat, despite the silly Marty Robbins tape they'd found among discarded rubbish. She'd sat at her desk comically popping her haunches as if mounted on a horse; Abe had obliviously kept shuffling photos and text on page three of the newsletter.

So she said to Cheryl, "Sure, I'd like to meet him."

2. Counter-turn

Contra-move 1.) "I've written you a love letter," he said.

"Really?" she brightened and bounced forward.

It was April First and he'd stayed late the day before to write a letter to a particularly recalcitrant female vice president who'd been their albatross all along. He'd come up with a new idea for a column about favorite pets, so that employees could "see one another as humans." This was inspired by the Christmas photo they'd used, a litter of kittens the plant had adopted thirty some years ago. He wanted Heloise's approval and signature for the new column. He'd signed the letter, "Love," and drawn a heart with a Smiley Face next to it.

When she read the letter, she looked up and glared briefly. She then sat at her computer, and they didn't talk for the remainder of the morning until she stood and made a motion with her fingers that she was going out to smoke. It dawned on Abe that she hadn't been smoking for the past month and he commented on that.

"I've started again," she said.

He followed her out, but her answers to his questions were guttural, monosyllabic. Maybe I should ask about her pets, he thought. Then he remembered that she lived in an apartment. "Did I ever tell you that I have two Dobermans?" he said, careful not to say the "we" that would indicate his wife.

"No."

They went back to work and then they went to their separate homes.

Contra-move 2.) After Judith did the taxes, she wanted to celebrate. She surprised Abe by suggesting they drive to Natural Bridge for a spring picnic. On the two-hour drive, Abe couldn't get Heloise out of his mind. She'd come from eastern Kentucky to the university, and as they passed through small hill towns he envisioned her standing with friends on a street corner, holding her arm askew the way she did to make some point or another. Since Judith was driving, he took out a poetry book and started reading. Judith was listening to a mystery. He was surprised at how relaxed he became and understood why Heloise enjoyed reading poetry. Judith herself surprised Abe when she agreed to hike the "moderate" trail up to the bridge, as opposed to the "easy" one. Friday, talking with Heloise he'd commented that his wife was from New York City and thought that anything beyond a block called for a cab.

"I love to hike," Heloise had responded. "I wanted to work with the Kentucky Trails Publishing Association, but by the time I graduated they'd filled the spot."

These surprises discombobulated Abe. His stomach turned the entire weekend.

Derby Day was looming and a fourth newsletter was nearly wrapped up. Abe toyed with the idea of inviting Heloise to go with him since someone had mentioned having tickets for sale. But then he realized that they'd have to spend the night in Louisville. How could he make an excuse to Judith?

Contra-move 3.) Wednesday before Derby he picked up their phone. It was Cheryl, Heloise's best friend, whose voice he'd come to recognize. He handed Heloise the phone and listened as Heloise kept naming someone named Terri. At first, that's what he thought, Terri with an 'i.' Then he realized that the Terry had a 'y' and that he was male. Heloise invited Cheryl over for a drink, saying that she and Terry weren't planning on going out, that they'd likely stay home.

The program he'd been using, Adobe Pagemaker, had been shutting down all morning because of "illegal operations." It was par for the program, but after overhearing the phone call he caught himself cursing loudly in four separate fits. At noon, Heloise started out the door, then walked back to almost come to attention beside his chair. He looked up at her chin, with its lovely dimple that fascinated him. "I hope your day gets better," she said. He blinked and answered thanks, and she walked out.

Immediately his day did get better, as long as he didn't think of Terry or the Derby. He went outside. In the parking lot he searched for Heloise's bright orange car. In the winter, she parked in the sunlight, and now in the summer, she parked in the shade. He spotted where she normally parked. It was empty; she'd likely driven to lunch. Why hadn't they ever gone to lunch together? He envisioned her rubbing her toe rings against Terry's calf at the nearby Pizza Hut. He stared at the empty slot, thinking of all the times Heloise had stood close enough that he could feel her body heat, if not her actual touch. He thought about the time that she had worn a new perfume that jolted him so much that he reached for her—but she'd jumped away. He thought about her saying, "This little girl wants someone she can kick around." He thought about her laughing at his purple stocking cap and threatening to buy one so that they could parade the halls as twins. He thought how he'd spotted Nietzsche's *Zarathustra* in her desk and now it dawned on him: she was reading Nietzsche because of him, just like he was reading poetry because of her. His stomach turned. A familiar feeling lately, though he hadn't felt it since his high school sweetheart left for Vanderbilt. He thought of walking inside and retrieving Heloise's poetry book. But he'd have to look in her private drawer. That tempted him. But what would he find? A snapshot of Terry? So he remained in the sunlight, having heard that was the best relief for depression.

Contra-move 4.) Three weeks after Derby Day, and June was on them. They'd been told that the June newsletter, their sixth, had to have two extra pages to push the company's softball league. Two extra pages, they explained to the female vice president, meant four extra pages because of the physical layout. "Fine," the v-p had replied, "we can run a large article on United Way and raise employee donations."

They walked back, solidified by their anger. She put in the Marty Robbins tape she was fond of and they sang "Big Iron," imagining an Arizona Ranger dropping into the plant to challenge the vice president to a gunfight. Blast her away. While singing, they hit shoulders and apologized simultaneously, which stopped their singing. Still, it seemed to him like matters were improving. Maybe Terry had moved on.

"Are you going to the party Friday? There's going to be a band, and free wine and beer. How can anyone pass that up? We may even get to chat with our friendly v-p." He emailed this to her on Wednesday. Judith was on one of her occasional Jewish upswings and had been going to the synagogue for the last two Friday evenings.

"Yeah." This was all she answered. He had to think what the question was.

He bit his lip. Besides the Marty Robbins song, they had another day where everything between them seemed as smooth as a tennis doubles' team, or as slick as a comic duo like Gracie Allen and George Burns. His parents had stuffed that duo down his throat until he grudgingly found comfort in their rhythmic comic patter . . . just as he found comfort in the rhythm of poetry. At any rate, Heloise and he hit stride a couple of days. One time he began addressing a plaster gorilla that they'd found, asking if it would please relay questions to Heloise, since she wasn't being receptive. She'd gotten into the game and relayed her answers through the gorilla, smacking it for emphasis and asking the gorilla to pass along a cuff if Abe didn't comprehend any multi-syllabic words. And there'd been another Grand Canyon smile between them both, hadn't there?

He went to the office party alone and looked for Heloise. He'd drunk three beers before he spotted her, standing next to some guy too tall to be real. So tall that he rested his elbow on her head.

"Abe! You still holed up with that good-looker over in the west section?"

Abe turned to see Francis Cox, a computer nerd he'd known since high school. Ol' Francis boy was making well over seventy grand, having graduated early and now working on his master's. Rumor had it that Francis was such a workaholic because his girlfriend and roommate had died within a week of one another in college. But they could have died on the same day and it wouldn't have bothered Frankie. He was a nerd asshole in Bardstown; now he was a nerd asshole in Lexington. He still drove the same egg blue Dodge pick-up he had in high school.

"No . . . yeah."

"Great! Input like that's just what I need for my fuzzy logic program. I'm combining fuzzy logic with game theory to imitate human decision-making, so computers can get a handle on matters. I call the program 'Lover's Paradox.' Inspired from all the crap in high school, you know?"

"Lover's Paradox?" Abe asked absently, seeing that the tall guy had removed his arm from Heloise's head. Had she told him to get it off? Had she grimaced like she had when he'd placed a desperate hand on her bare shoulder three days ago? *I . . . I want to love you and touch you*, he'd thought. *Get your damned hand off my bare back*, she'd thought.

"Yeah, all the love-me, hate-you stuff. Just like high school. Just like everyone at this party." Frankie boy was drinking Coke and he tipped it against Abe's beer. "I got drunk once in college," he observed. "How do people stand it? Give me caffeine or . . ." his eyes shifted to spot a nearby supervisor. Frankie shrugged, "Give me caffeine any day."

Abe nodded. Presumably Francis was going to say 'cocaine,' but then maybe he was just going to say, 'a computer screen.' Peripherally, Abe saw Heloise and the too-tall guy, their hips touching. Feeling his stomach churn he dropped his lukewarm beer into a red garbage barrel, imagining himself butting it over like a bull. He left the party.

Contra-move 5.) The next Monday, Heloise told him that she got wild and was singing Janis Joplin onstage with the band just before midnight. He imagined her thin body shivering with each bluesy note.

"I wish I'd seen you. I wish . . ." He stopped, thinking of his dad's satirical response to such phrases: "If wishes were horses, beggars would ride."

"I wish," he continued, despite himself and his dad.

"Yeah," Heloise replied. "It was great fun. I saw you talking with the geek."

"Cox?"

"Yeah. What's he doing, making programs that can procreate?"

Abe told her about Lover's Paradox. She nodded vaguely, looking out the perverted, high windows.

"I've got something to tell you," she said.

Abe stared at the gorilla, thinking of walking over and giving it a kiss or a love squeeze.

"I've asked for a transfer to another department. It's more money, more stable. I'll get to travel. Our friend the vice president wants me to stay another week and help you finish this newsletter."

Later, when he was sitting at the computer and she was standing nearby proofreading, he reached to touch her bare shoulder. Again, the same stupid thing that had pissed her off a week ago. But maybe it was okay, considering. "I'll miss you," he said.

She inhaled and removed his hand. "I'll miss working here."

So she was leaving. This news came before the July Fourth holiday, so he didn't see her Monday. Tuesday she called and told him she had a doctor's appointment.

"Heloise," he said on Wednesday, when she walked in.

"Hey," she replied dully.

Contra-move 6.) Feeling his throat catch, he leaned against the door and bolted it. She was already at the computer. If she noticed or heard him bolting the door, she didn't indicate. He'd sequestered himself from his wife the night before and he'd written something he'd never written before, a love poem. He handed it to Heloise. She didn't look up from her purse. It was a new one, compact and red patent leather with gold catches. Where was her simple cotton purse? He missed it.

"Do you want me to read this now?" she asked.

Once more his throat caught, and when it did, she looked up. He nodded.

His Second Love Poem to Her

His second, though he never gave her a first;
His second, because he wanted to try twice,
knowing it could never be worse;
His second, because minutes, hours and days
slipped away;
His second, because thing-filled things had
claimed his first;

His second, because he wanted a third to slake
    his thirst;
His second, because she was leaving, and only
    good-bye remained;
His second, because he wished, he wished, he
    wished he'd given her a first.

She folded the poem carelessly, and he could tell that she only folded it because he was standing there expecting her to tuck it away in that lovely striped cotton purse as a memento. But the lovely striped cotton purse wasn't anymore. It was patent leather red, filled with the passion of moving.

"I have to go," she said, pushing her chair back. "I've got errands. I'll just take a personal leave day."

His hand twitched, wanting to touch her, hold her. But she already went by him and was opening the double door, where he hoped she would turn. But she didn't. She undid the latch with a snap. Then door closed and there he stood.

He imagined the poem falling out of the red purse when she unlocked her car. He imagined it flipping against her new ruby ankle bracelet. He imagined it being caught in the wind and turning, counter-turning, and turning away.

3. Stand

Some weeks later, they both had an arid August dream about a shelf. The wood for this shelf was rough, as if hewn with an adze outside a cave in firelight, while creatures just beyond the pale stared with hooded eyes. In the dream, sunlight streamed in, only revealed as sunlight because of dust motes in the barren room. If one tiptoed, splits running the shelf's grain became apparent. It must have undergone severe changes of heat and cold, aridity and moisture, over an untold period of time. One could imagine the shelf eventually dropping off the wall into awaiting dust motes. In their separate dreams, they both saw the shelf bowing upward, as if reaching for the ineffable. But it was empty. And it stayed empty. Perhaps it had never held any weight whatsoever, like a grand, uneven canyon, once cut by effusive water, now gouged only with time.

The Breakdown Club

"Tigers." Tim stared at a yellow-green, retractable metal ruler he'd just retrieved from behind the pick-up's seat. "They can't see any colors, only a yellow-green haze." It was early morning, the metal was cold, and no response came to his statement.

At a zoo several years before, Tim and a woman he'd lived with entered a concrete hut to gaze through tinted Plexiglas at two tigers. The Plexiglas's purpose was to let onlookers momentarily experience what the paired tigers—who possessed no functional color cones—saw: pervasive yellow-green. Suddenly one tiger crouched—at what, neither Tim nor the woman, whose warm bare shoulder rubbed his, could figure out. The tiger remained alert and crouched, its tail quivering, until they left the hut. Tim had oddly deduced that if tigers can't see true colors, then they can't see the past. If they can't see the past, where does that leave the future? Three months later, in no causal connection he'd ever been able to identify, he and the woman separated.

The pick-up roared to life as his boss finished a sip of coffee. Tim patted the pick-up's dash and wished it well—a not foolish notion, considering the yellow-green morning. Pulling the ruler open, he confirmed inches and centimeters, the possibility of feet and meters.

His boss, in a mood, flipped on the radio. Vapor spewed from surround-sound speakers to cloy Tim's nostrils—country music, hip-hop? Whatever, it would be impolite to complain, so leaning

Joe Taylor

back he drank his own coffee. With a third yellow-green sip he tried to remember last night, thinking maybe he'd been sucker-punched in a fight or maybe fallen drunkenly. But no, he'd stayed home. Had he slipped in the shower, then? A head trauma would explain this yellow-green. He could consult the Oliver Sacks guy from TV about primate emotions resulting from bi-chromatic vision. Monochromatic?

He did remember talking with Cheryl last night, on the phone. He'd first met her eight months before at The Breakdown Club, the bar everyone went to. She streaked her hair blonde. Sandy brown, really. She cooked at The Club and went to a tanning salon bi-weekly. . . . On the phone, had they argued? Tim closed his eyes, but she appeared as a yellow-green image. Which wasn't too bad. This bi- or mono-chromism, once you got used to it, wasn't too bad. Cheryl's teeth, for instance, still smiled. And her eyes and mouth—what did they do?

The truck purred to a stop. Tim rubbed his nose against a cool window and looked at a newly forming subdivision—decked out in yellow-green, of course. *It'll be okay,* he whispered to the window, nearly kissing it. Opening the door he walked toward a garage, snapping the tape measure. This morning, they were going to pour a concrete driveway. He'd float and level, finish, go home, either call Cheryl or not, go to sleep or not, and wake up to a new day and birds singing. Or not.

Then things slipped. A half-naked black in his late-teens, early twenties, stood in the garage holding a shovel they'd evidently forgotten yesterday. All the forms they'd measured and nailed into place were splintered.

"What the fuck!"

The kid stepped toward Tim, his eyes glaring black-brown and drug-ridden. He swung the shovel hard enough that he nearly toppled, banging it against the garage's cinder block wall to give off sparks. Tim heard Walter, his boss, crunching gravel behind. As the kid took a swing at Walter, Tim maneuvered to kick the back of the kid's left knee, toppling him into gravel. But the kid was on his feet immediately, now gripping the shovel mid-way like a fighting stick. Taking quick steps he connected with Tim's bottom finger. Tim dropped the ruler and threw what remained of his coffee into the kid's face while Walter hit the kid over the head with a broken two-by-four from their messed-up framing job. Tim's finger stung like hell but he stepped into the kid's path and smashed his face with his right palm, trying for the nose but connecting with the left cheek. He then bunched his hurt hand into a shaky fist and hit with the kid's nose just as Walter once more connected with the kid's skull. This sent the kid to his knees outside the garage, so Tim kicked him in the stomach and Walter once more hit him—on the shoulders this time.

The kid flopped.

"Mother fucker!" Tim grabbed his stinging finger and whirled to deliver another kick, this time to the kid's face with his right work boot. This sent the kid scrambling for something in his pants pocket, so Walter, a big man, slammed down with the two-by, and the scrambling stopped.

Tim held off from kicking again to suck in air and look to Walter, then to his pinkie, which was gashed and dripping blood from where the shovel had connected. He kicked the shovel away and stared at the black kid, whose eyes remained open. Pink spittle oozed from the kid's mouth. Tim squeezed his hand and yelled, "Mother fucker!" again.

"He's dead," Walter said, moving around to face the kid on the ground.

"Good."

"It was just a two-by-four," Walter said, bending warily.

But the kid wasn't dead and he lunged for Walter, toppling him and crawling on top to bite Walter's face.

Tim delivered a hard kick to the kid's ass, trying for his nuts. Another. Then he grabbed the two-by-four and began walloping the kid's back, producing instant welts, even on black skin. He finally got a clear shot at his head and hit it twice, breaking the two-by with the second hit, then lunging to lodge the broken sliver loosely in the kid's neck.

Walter rolled away and picked up the shovel, jumping to his feet and swinging it downward to connect with the wooden sliver; but instead of driving deeper, the sliver exited taking a chunk of flesh and leaving blood spurting an inch or so into cool air. Walter staggered back. Tim saw a red oval on Walter's cheek and another on his brow, where the kid had bitten him. Squeezing his left hand, Tim looked to see that blood was no longer spurting from the gash in the kid's neck. So this time he *was* dead.

Walter called 911 on his cell phone. Then he called to cancel the concrete, but the truck was already on its way.

Holding his gashed finger near his stomach, Tim bent to pat the kid's pocket, the one he'd been reaching for. A clump of metal, probably a knife. Two flecks of gray gravel stuck to the kid's open and very dead eye.

Something sounded from inside the nearly completed house. He and Walter went to the truck to grab a three-foot scrap of metal rebar and a crowbar; then they walked to the back of the house. Someone had kicked in the sliding glass door and had shit on the floor.

"I smell something," Tim said.

"Crackhead shit," Walter responded as they stepped inside.

"No. Perfume."

Walter sniffed and winced from the bite on his cheek.

"Smell it?"

Walter nodded. They skirted the mound of shit and followed a line of dark-brown urine along unfinished plasterboard leading from the kitchen to the hall. It reminded Tim of a graph from high school math. More of the kid's handiwork, no doubt. The perfume became stronger.

She sat huddled on the floor with a blue tarp around her, probably stolen from a nearby work site. She glared when they entered and scrambled for a CD player amid a pile of clothing, crackers, chips, and candy to come up with something silvery in her right hand.

"Whoa! Whoa! It's okay. What's your name?"

"Where's Hot Time?" she asked.

"Hot Time?"

"My friend. Where is he?"

Walter and Tim looked to one another and hid the makeshift weapons behind their backs.

"A black guy?"

It wasn't metal she held but a CD, and she was now fighting a purple CD player. She angrily flipped the CD against a far wall. Tim shifted and through a window could see the dead kid on the gravel.

"You two got something against blacks?" she asked, drawing Tim back.

"How old is he, this Hot Time?"

"Thirty, forty." She stared at another CD in her hand and tried to get the player to take it, but it wouldn't. "Seventeen, ten. No, he can get a wallop hard-on, so seventeen. You two want blowjobs? Twenty bucks apiece. I got the best tongue in the county." She stuck out her tongue to reveal two silver balls. Her teeth were spotted yellow and brown. "Why you care how old he is? I'm plenty legal, if that's what you're thinking. So . . . twenty bucks apiece? Unless one of you can get this friggin' CD player to work, then it drops to ten."

Walter's cell phone rang and she scooted backwards.

"You're not going to believe it," Walter spoke into the phone. He mouthed, "Frank and Joe" to Tim and gestured toward the girl on the floor with a shrug and a roll of his blue eyes. Tim could see watery plasma draining from the bite on Walter's cheek. Walter turned to the girl and started to say something, but thought better of it and just walked out, again telling Frank that he wasn't going to believe what happened and to, yeah, come on over anyway.

Tim and the girl were alone. Tim propped the metal rebar outside the door.

"My name's Tim"

"I got a boyfriend."

"Hot Time?"

"Hot Time's a nigger. A dealer."

"What's your name?"

She stopped fighting the CD player long enough to look up. Then she studied the CD in her hand, which began to tremble. "I . . . I don't know." She dropped the CD and ran her fingers through the mess on the floor, coming up with a broken cigarette. She stared at it for a minute, then looked up. "You got a light?"

Tim produced a lighter, leaning toward her. She brushed his hand away when it approached her lips but then grabbed his wrist to bring it and the light near. She exhaled at the CD player. "Piece of shit wasn't worth stealin'." She kicked it. Tim could hear Walter outside on the back patio, still explaining to Frank on the phone.

"Hey you. Green eyes," she said. "Come here and let me suck your big cock for twenty bucks. I'm hungry and need some hot protein soup."

"Look, your friend Hot Time had something happen to him. You need to get out of here."

"Twenty bucks and then I'm gone like The History Channel, you know?" She sucked on the half-cigarette, exaggerating her lips into fish-kisses. She tried to blow a stream of smoke at Tim but coughed most of it out. Dressed in a male's green silk shirt, probably Hot Time's, she stretched to reveal her right breast, which showed a dark nipple nearly as large as the entire breast.

Tim pulled out his wallet and took out a twenty, trembling when pain shot through his pinkie. "Here, take it and the lighter and go on and leave. You need to get out of this house. It isn't yours."

"I shit a sacred Egyptian pyramid in it last night. It's mine."

"No it isn't. You need to leave." Tim heard the concrete truck coming up the road and saw Walter run in the gravel to wave frantically at the driver. The dead kid still lay twisted. Tim pushed the twenty near the cigarette, but the girl slapped it away.

"I'm not a freak beggar. I work for my money." She flipped the cigarette against a wall and reached to tug his zipper down. He pulled back, but she clung to his blue jeans and whined,

"Lisa's hungry. She needs hot protein soup."

"That's your name, Lisa?"

She blinked. Her eyes must have been brilliant blue once, though they now looked like gray, slushy snow. "I . . . maybe. I think so." On her knees, she fell into him. Her hair was bleached, but still soft. He stroked it like she was a puppy and kept his pinkie behind his back. Oddly, she started purring, and her mouth was incredibly warm and soft. She ran the silver balls along his major vein and began humming something he couldn't place, though the vibration against his cock riveted him.

Looking outside, he saw Walter gesturing toward the dead kid and talking with a huge black driver named Marx. People swore they'd seen Marx lift a full barrel of water and carry it twenty yards.

"Hungry. Feed Darla. Feed her, blue-eyed man."

"Darla," Tim started, tensing.

"Peggy. Feed Paula." She looked up, rubbing his cock from cheek to cheek, then sniffing its head with her nose, stuffing it in each nostril, as if she might inhale it. Then she took it in her mouth again and began humming.

Two minutes later, Tim felt himself exploding. Making exaggerated swallows, she pressed against him, causing him to stumble back, though she clasped his ass to steady him and kept running the two silver balls over his penis. Leaning, he saw a pink thong riding her pale crack, where her dress had slipped. On her right buttock were two parallel cigarette burns over an inch long. She was sucking and inhaling deeply now, and he was certain she was having an orgasm. She dug two fingers into his sac, then fell backward to spread her legs and rub herself and gyrate her hips, watching him and licking her lips.

"Sandy. Paula. Alice."

Outside, Marx gunned the mixer to keep the concrete from setting up. The young woman yelped and stopped gyrating. Pulling her hand from her vagina she offered it. Tim leaned but she laughed and stuck it in her mouth and slurped, then wiped her fingers in her hair. Scooting toward him by bouncing her hips, she twittered her fingers. He blinked.

"My . . . my twenty."

He spotted it on the floor where it had fallen, and he picked it up and gave it to her. "You need to go. Now. Police will be coming."

With a grunt she gathered what candy and chips were left into a greasy sack, then kicked the CD player with a curse and stood. She pulled her silk shirt away to reveal her right breast, again with that dark nipple. "Men tell me it's like honey-sugar."

When she stepped toward him, Tim could see not a nipple but a large scab.

"You need to go. Police."

She laughed and pulled up her loose skirt, then ran out the bedroom door. He followed her into the kitchen, past the mound of shit, but stopped before leaving the house, noticing her bare feet on the cold concrete.

He shouted, "Here!" She turned and he held out another twenty.

She spat at him, a yellow-green gob hitting his wrist.

Then she was running across a field five or six lots wide toward another new house. A car sat parked beside it, one he hadn't noticed when they'd pulled in. In the waist-high yellow grass her skirt billowed yellow-green as a breeze swept in, or maybe something in her gait stirred the blades as her haunches shifted. Suddenly she was down, as if jumped by a predator. He could see the pelt on her back twitching where her silk shirt was ripped. Had it been ripped before? Clutching the frame of the broken sliding glass door, he spotted a police car with lights flashing, no siren. After it passed and made a turn, she stood bi-pedal and erect on the veldt, cupping her right ear preternaturally. Her haunches shifted and she ran to the car, falling against it as if struck from behind with a large stone. She fought the door and soon Tim heard the car's engine cough hoarsely. The beast, a stegosaurus, tore backwards over newly laid sod. Tim half-heartedly raised his throbbing hand to wave, half-heartedly hoping she was watching the rear view mirror.

But she wouldn't be. What could she ever find useful in a monochrome past? His finger throbbed and he heard Walter yell for him. The landscape shifted to a false technicolor as the girl and her blue Honda Accord drove off.

"I'm here," Tim yelled back, realizing that he was.

The Man Who Haunted
Himself

During the first era when we journeyed to procure the tombstones
. . . well, I need to be careful, for I was going to claim that the whole
affair of living was simpler then, but maybe I should just note that
it was more orderly. The route—we pronounced that word "root"
at the time, as if it offered a thing we could clasp, a thing that
would grow unto us, as opposed to "rout," a thing that would drive
us outside ourselves—the route to the tombstones always remained
placid and clear. First, you swam the fluid toward the Great
Crevasse, and then keeping the Three Angelic Rocks in your sight,
you swam to them, and then began your ascent upward from the
Great Crevasse until you reached a hoary outgrowth resembling
a lip, whereupon it became necessary to forsake the fluid and
walk along a grassy meadow—its grass casting off a brilliant and
luxurious green—until you spotted the towering trees.

They weren't Sequoias, though nearly as large. Their bark was
smoother, more like a sweetgum or sycamore. When you reached
them, all you needed to do was follow their canopy until you found
Joe's log cabin, which sat off the path, far back—at least a hundred
yards—in a clearing. In spring this clearing glowed with yellow
dandelions; in summer, profusely green grass and good luck clover;
in winter, colorful mustard greens, which anyone might cook up
and eat, grew in profusion. Fall? Ah, fall brought goldenrod, which
made me sneeze.

Inside that cabin, Joe carved tombstones. He was assigned the job because of his parents and because of his red hair. I know these don't seem sufficient reasons, but it's what everyone said and no one ever claimed different. So I won't attempt changing facts now, especially when it's become so hellishly hard to procure them—the tombstones, I mean. That's what I'm talking about.

It was always Terry and me who swam for the tombstones, and it was always Frances who sent us, just ahead of necessity. Women, I think, have a feel for such things.

"It's time for some tombstones," she might say.

Or maybe, "Tonight, instead of stopping for pigs' feet and beer, you and Terry need to visit Joe The Tombstone Maker."

And off Terry and me would go.

"Terri's a woman's name," I'd sometimes kid him. We'd be swimming in the fluid, inhaling its sweetness without really paying attention, and he'd break his infamous breaststroke to reach down and grab a gob of seaweed or muck to throw at me. Easy to avoid, since throwing anything in the fluid was difficult.

"There's women named Sammy too," he'd counter. We had to stay close to hear one another in the fluid, but staying close seemed to come natural then.

"Prove it. Name one," I dared him.

"Sammie," he'd say, whipper-snappery petulant.

"Sammie what?"

Of course he could never come up with a family name.

Once one of us said, just as we were nearing the Three Angelic Rocks and spotted a school of shiny green fish about twice the size of our palms: "I heard of a man named Francis." We immediately held our fluid breaths until our ears pounded from the pressure. That's one sure thing about the Three Angelic Rocks: they mark the lowest point on the journey and the consequent fluid pressure can build up almost dangerously, depending upon temperature and season.

"Francis," I sighed, in affirmation. Or maybe it was Terry who sighed, I'm not sure. Because even though it was Frances and me who were lovers, I always suspected that Terry had an eye out for her too. Who can blame him? With her skin so smooth and tan—even at the height of the gray season when the fluid flows densest around our villages and houses. With her gums so young and laughing, her teeth so shiny. With her vast eyes emerald and piercing, her joints that shift with each pronouncement rendering it a laugh, not a burden. . . . It's clear how much she meant to me, as clear as the fluid about us in winter. Or, at least, as clear as the fluid used to be. It's clear how much she *means* to me, I meant to write. I meant to mean.

Which is what I'm coming to.

"It's time for you and Terry to go fetch some grave markers," Frances said one day when I came home for lunch. Actually, I had come home for some afternoon delight. Frances and I had planned it as a "surprise" for one another, a romp in the garden of lily love to forget work's drudge. She'd just gotten our last girl in day school and could concentrate on her pottery; I'd just gotten a promotion and supervised all the special fluid-proof boxes under two-foot square. Stamped them each and every with my name: *Sammy's crew.*

"Grave markers?" I asked. "What are, what is, what . . . do you mean tombstones?"

"Well sure," she replied.

The signs were there, if I'd been willing to look. First, just the idea of planning a surprise is weird enough. And then Frances calling them grave markers instead of tombstones, well that pounded the old nail in the coffin, so to speak.

"It's Joe that still makes them, isn't it?" I asked, mentally measuring her hips as she leaned against a counter and reached for glassware. She looked over her shoulder with her emerald eyes, but the light caught wrong and they showed yellow brown. Her teeth still glowed with that same smile though; I assured myself of this as I watched her pull down two glasses.

"It is, isn't it? Joe, I mean?"

She set the glasses on the counter and filled them with a heavy spring beer. Pouring fluid inside the fluid could take place two ways—easy to figure when you thought about it. You either poured up or you poured out, depending upon whether the fluid was lighter or heavier than what you wanted to put in the container. This beer—this afternoon delight beer—was heavier than the fluid, so Frances poured it down and it displaced the fluid. Specific gravity, it's called, to be—ha-ha—specific. Frances extended her lovely tanned arm and one of the beers to me.

"To afternoon delight," she said. Her eyes almost glowed emerald green and her shoulders almost laughed as she raised her beer. Our glasses clink-clunked in the oceanic way that things did in the fluid, and one of her sharp nails snipped a piece of flesh from my ring finger.

She hadn't answered my question about Joe. Did he still make the tombstones, these grave markers, or not? It had been a while since Terry and I had last swum for some—an half-dozen that time, so it was a difficult journey, even knowing the way. And three of those were smaller tombstones. Those are always the hardest, aren't they, the small ones? As if any of them are easy.

Frances shifted her hips through the fluid toward me and I forgot about Joe the tombstone carver as she pushed me down, right on the walnut floor of the dining room, right in the middle of a patch of yellow sunlight filtering down. Is seminal fluid heavier than the fluid? This marked the first time I ever wondered that. Should Frances be tilting me up, or should I be tilting her down? My hand rubbed her thin belly afterwards, wondering, wondering.

"Two," she said.

For a moment, thinking of sperm and seminal fluid, I thought she meant twins. Then I remembered the tombstones.

"Two grave markers," she whispered in my ear, as if aligning my thoughts toward the latest idiom.

So that afternoon, since summertime still held a nice yellow light, Terry and I stopped for a beer before swimming for the . . .

"Grave markers? What are . . ."

Terry asked the same question I had, so I explained about tombstones now being called grave markers. He stared out the window of the bar. "Joe said it's the weight of the tombstone that's important. Two hundred pounds minimum pegs people in place, keeps them from floating up and haunting themselves."

"Themselves?"

"That's what he said."

"You've actually seen Joe?" This intrigued me, because as many times as I'd been to his shop, I'd never seen him: the tombstones were always sitting in the middle of the ivory linoleum floor, waiting. And I always left our small gramercy.

Terry pointed out the bar's window. Clumps of seaweed slapped against the pane, and a pink anemone slapped there, too, like it was a kid's face smushed and spying on us and the other customers in the bar. "Sea's shifting in," Terry said.

"No way, it's too—" But I turned and saw that he was right: the yellow was being replaced with a blue gray.

"We'd better hurry."

We left the bar. Thirty minutes later, we were halfway to the Three Angelic Rocks, a distance that an abandoned stucco house informally marks. It used to be a tavern, at least that's what I remember, since I was always too young to go in, though I can still picture a tall blonde-haired woman walking out and leaning hard on a man named Frank one day. "That's Sammie," my dad had told me. "I used to go out with her until I met your mom." Wait. Were Dad and I swimming or walking? I can see the blonde woman's long ivory legs—were her feet shod in red heels or red rubber flippers? It gets tough remembering the past, with all the tombstones . . . with all the grave markers. Anyway, why would a dad tell his kid something like that? Was he sad that he didn't still "go out with her"? Was he happy that he stopped? Did he love my mom?

Sammie. The name dawned on me. Sammie with an "ie," not with a "y." But damn me if I was going to tell Terry.

Then the oddest thing: the stucco tavern was open when we

reached it.

"Look, someone's revamped the old place and opened it," I announced, nudging Terry as we swam along.

He stopped stroking the fluid to stare at me. " 'Salways been open, Sammy," he said. "Geesh. Want to stop for another beer?"

I checked my watch and appraised the blue gray fluid moving toward us.

"Come on, we got time. All we got to get is two—"

"Grave markers," I finished for him, feeling an unlucky tinge lying about the word *tombstones* now that we weren't using it.

From the tavern's door swam the aroma of bacon, mixed with undertones of whiskey and beer mash. And inside, the gray pulsing waves seemed heavier, though there were plenty of windows, some open and so allowing the fluid to pass freely. I could see eels slipping in and out the back window near a gaming machine. I was surprised, for eels usually kept their distance, especially these blue lampreys.

I smelled perfume and someone grabbed my arm.

It was Sammie. I mean, I guess she was Sammie, just like I remembered her from the time I'd seen her as a kid. Maybe it was her daughter. I bit my lip before offering the question, "Sammie?"

"My soul mate," she sighed, and that sigh burbled out her perfume; it filled my nostrils to make me wonder whether sighs were heavier than the fluid, whether I should tilt myself up or down to breathe one in.

2.

My father used to claim—with the frequency of blinking—"You just never can tell what will cause what in this world, or what has been caused by what." My mother would roll her gray-blue eyes and send him to fetch three or two or four tombstones. All the time I lived at home, I thought how my father was stupider than the sea urchins we had to avoid stepping on. Now I think . . . well, now is now.

After leaving the tavern, Terry and I were walking—walking!

And the Three Angelic Rocks still lay a fair way in the distance, down in a valley where haze was forming. I sighed, and realized that this was a repeat gesture. Now that we were evidently in air, what about the weight of sighs? Up, or down?

Terry croaked out a laugh and said, "Don't worry, Sammy. All bipeds are sad after they fuck."

"What—"

"Don't even bother to deny it. You and Sammie's faces was flushed like bands on a coral snake when you walked down the stairs, and you only drank three beers, so alcohol wasn't causing it. Besides," and here Terry pointed to his thin nose, which resembled a fish's spine, "besides, I could smell cum on you both. Shot off a wad, didn't ya?"

I gazed away at the bluish haze. Had there once been decorum? When tombstones were tombstones, I mean? When the fluid was fluid?

We walked on, and instead of whale song, we heard birdsong. Pleasant enough, don't get me wrong, but where's the resonance? Gone as soon as it comes, birdsong.

Being dirt-bound and air-immersed offered other challenges. Twice we had to backtrack when we lost sight of the Three Angelic Rocks and took a wrong path. And once we did reach them, the climb upward was much more arduous than the swimming ascent we formerly made. The easing air pressure didn't seem to matter at all: I mean that there were no expanding gasses in our lungs and blood vessels to buoy us upward, to speed us along.

"Ga," Terry exclaimed, stepping on a spiky sycamore seed and falling against a tree.

Some things never change; instead of sea urchins, sycamore seeds. But then I registered with dismay the sycamore tree that had shed the seed, for we hadn't yet reached the lip where we normally forsook the fluid for the trees and grasses. Now here stood a tree already. And something other than a hurt foot was bothering Terry, too.

"Shouldn't of drunk that last beer. Should of found me a Terri to tarry with."

"But then you'd be sad," I said.

"Huh?"

"*Post copulum, omne animal sunt triste.*"

"What's that mean?"

"After fucking, all bipeds—"

"Oh yeah."

Decorum. It's gone. A robin landed in another tree and sang. It wasn't much, a two-tone ditty, but it got us moving again. Terry kept hobbling and rubbing his foot until we reached and passed over the hoary lip. For some reason, his foot healed as we started down the road leading to Joe the grave-marker maker's. My father would simply have shaken his head about Terry's healed foot and said, "Told you. Can't ever tell what will cause what."

"Told you," I informed Terry.

"Huh?"

Terry was right about one thing: I could smell sex on my body. I thought about Frances and our afternoon delight just five hours ago. So why in the tavern had I . . . the perfume? The red toenail polish? The Parisian lips? Somehow, the source of my miserable mistake reeled back to the tombstone/grave marker word-shift. Was my indescretion and that word-shift connected? My father wouldn't have been surprised.

"I don't think we're on the right path. I mean, where's the canopy of . . . whatever they were. Are."

It wouldn't surprise me at all if we were lost. Did I say that to Terry, or just think it? Whichever, Terry pressed my right arm and pointed to a grassy field littered with hunks of what looked like huge rotting sea turtles, whose carapaces had been painted a multiplicity of colors. *Johnny's Auto Salvage*, a sign faded to chalk-blue read.

"There's women named Johnnie," Terry noted, apropos of the sign.

I didn't ask him to name one. Then I saw the faux sequoias and the red tombstone—grave marker! Those indicated Joe's was just three hundred yards ahead.

I pointed it out. "Visit Joe's," I joked. This resembled the same tired jokes Terry and I exchanged every time we passed that marker. "Souvenirs? Stop at Joe's!" "Feets needs a rest? Stop at Joe's!" "You can't miss Joe's any more than it can miss you!" "Drop off the kids!" Though that one hadn't been so funny the time we came for the half-dozen tombstones.

So we walked on, giving wide berth to *Johnny's Auto Salvage*.

The road to Joe's—actual Sequoias now? And I didn't remember it having all this dusty red clay that rose to fill my nostrils, though I figured that would wash out once we got back into the fluid. Then I remembered that the Three Angelic Rocks lay behind us in an air pocket valley. Air, air, everywhere, and not a drop to drink. Were we ever going to return to the fluid? I pictured Frances's eyes earlier in the afternoon, how they'd looked almost yellow instead of emerald. When I raised my leg or arm or some body part, I smelled Sammie's perfume and sex musk, and I hit my forehead in anger.

"Look!" Terry said.

Another tavern.

"No way. We're not stopping there. That last one caused enough—"

"Look, Mr. Fucked-But-Sad, how's about I get my chance?"

I nodded, so in we walked. This time there was no mistaking the smell of bacon, but oddly I smelled seaweed too. Were they serving those new-fangled algae-burgers? Terry veered off toward a woman I didn't recognize and they immediately rubbed their hips together. Well, no sense in wasting time.

I walked up to a bar made of oak so old that it had darkened to mahogany. The bartender was polishing a martini glass. Her hips were thin, like Frances's, though I couldn't make out her face in the mirror because of all the liquor bottles and cigar humidors.

"Cabernet?" she asked. "We have a special vintage. Fifty-eight years old."

"How'd you—" I mean, I didn't even know. I thought I was

going to order a beer, but a cabernet, especially a cabernet that was just my age, fit right in, more . . . decorous.

She turned to hand me the wine. It was Frances. I could of just looked at her hands and known, but I saw her smile and her eyes. Her gums weren't as cherry red as they used to be, and her left front tooth had a glow to it, like maybe it was false. Her eyebrows had always been thin, but when did she stop wearing mascara? Really, her eyes had always been so large and beautiful that mascara almost detracted anyway.

"You look good," I said, stupidly.

She smiled her Frances smile, though it had a tinge now, like an Indian statue of Buddha, maybe. But then Buddhas don't really smile, do they? Before I could pinpoint just what the difference was, before she could smell Sammie's perfume and sex on me— though maybe the bacon, cigar smoke, and algae burgers would cover that—before she could, though, I asked,

"It's been bugging me. Why the change from tombstones to grave markers? I mean why this afternoon. Why?"

"*This* afternoon? *Why?*" She smiled, concentrating on a beer she was pulling from a tap for another customer. It was dark red, I thought, shaking my head, almost blood red. She carried it to the customer and marked down his tab. Then she came back to stand before me, popping her heels together in the way she had of using her body to get attention.

"*That* afternoon was thirty-two years ago. On Chantilly Street. Why are you worried about it now?"

"Thirty . . . Chantilly." I looked at her hands: wrinkles and age spots. A jagged scar I didn't recognize on a finger, like she'd cut it badly with a can lid or something else with rough edges. Cigar smoke drifted between us and she whiffed, her nose making the cute crinkle that I always loved so much. Always, always. She leaned back and pulled two bottles of whiskey off a glass shelf in front of the huge mirror. In it, I saw my face: my hair was white and had taken on a curl I didn't recognize. My brows were furrowed from too much sun. My eyebrows, they were white, too. Still handsome,

I assured myself. Then I saw age spots on my forehead. A young woman in her twenties walked up to my left and ordered a drink. When Frances asked for her ID the girl glanced at me, crinkled her nose and leaned away as she pulled the ID from her purse. She was holding her breath. Could she smell cum on me?

"Is this the way to Joe the grave marker maker's?" I asked after Frances had finished serving the girl, whose 21st had come five months ago.

"That sounds like the start of a joke," Frances replied. "But yes, it's right on the way. Joe's is right next door."

"Does he still have all that red hair?" I asked.

She shrugged and seemed more interested in finding another martini glass to polish.

As hard as she studied the martini glass, I studied my face in the mirror. Of a sudden, I knew at least one name that was going to be on the two grave markers. Frances could see that I figured that out because she rubbed her finger along the glass, making it ring.

"Thirty-two pounds isn't much to hold a ghost down."

"Beg your pardon?" She didn't look up from the martini glass.

"Grave markers only weigh about thirty-two pounds these days. No heft like a real tombstone."

She shrugged and placed the glass back in the rack.

"I'm sorry," I said. "Thirty-two years, I mean."

"It was hard finding Joe's place that evening," she offered.

I nodded and took a sip of the cabernet. It was acidic, bitter, but I let that go. Maybe it was just my aging taste buds.

"A lot of things, they got in your way," she offered, still concentrating on the newest martini glass.

I nodded again. Then, to prevent her from making further excuses for me, I asked, "How are the two girls?"

"Four."

I looked up sharply.

"I had twins. One of them was hurt coming out—my hips, you

know." She glanced down at her small hips.

I placed my palms on the bar and pressed as if I could see through it to her lower body.

"She died four years ago. The other hasn't been the same."

"I'm sorry," I said.

"I'm sorry," she echoed.

"Wanna see a bar trick?" This came from a woman in her late twenties, with blonde hair, almost a Sammie, I thought.

"No."

"Yes."

"Yes," I agreed, nodding at Frances's insistence.

"I'll need—"

But Frances had already placed a glass of clear water before the young woman. A crone, helping the beauteous new and upcoming village shaman. When the young woman reached for a bar swizzle stick, I noted her thin hips, her angular joints. In the space before the mirror where the two whiskey bottles had been, I could make out the bulge of her eyes, like Frances's. Maybe this woman was older than her mid-twenties, maybe she was early thirties, even maybe she was my . . . but when I looked to Frances for a clue, she was paying me no heed, she was simply tilting her head and watching the girl.

Who promptly picked out a nude male swizzle stick and dropped it in the water, whereupon it promptly sank. She looked at me for affirmation, and I inhaled, seeing her emerald eyes. She tapped the glass to draw my attention back to the trick.

"So?" I asked.

"Heavier than water, right? A lot heavier than water."

"Specific gravity," I said.

"Specific gravity, yeah, yeah. My granddad said that we—that humans—used to swim in what he called the fluid." She shook her head, keeping her eye on the nude male swizzle stick, which seemed to be yellowing in the water, but surely that was a trick of the bar lighting. The guy with the cigar walked by again, puffing it between the young woman and me.

"Seen it before," he said, walking off.

"Old people are too stupid to realize what's right before them." The girl addressed this to his back—and for some reason I shrank her age down to girlhood. "So they either act like they've traveled the world and seen it all, or they make up bullshit like my granddad did. The fluid. Like we lived in some amniotic haven." She snorted.

Frances's father, my father-in-law, had been alive thirty-two years before, as healthy as a boar hog, and he always snorted his laughs out like one. I looked up at Frances, but she put a finger to her lips.

"Hey! Think I can make this stud float?" the girl asked.

I shrugged, trying to catch something of me in her.

"Bet me. Just a drink. It's worth that, right?"

I shrugged again and said, "Sure," when Frances's fingernail hit the bar.

Again, Frances the crone began assisting the new and upcoming shaman. Frances set down a draught beer in a pilsner glass. The girl plucked the nude male swizzle stick from the water and dropped it into the beer. Before it hit bottom, bubbles were adhering to it.

"The bubbles," I half-laughed, thinking how they used to help us ascend from the Three Angelic Rocks.

Then something odd happened: the male swizzle stud began to not only yellow but to crumble. His right hand floated upward. Then his over-sized phallus. A leg. The left side of his face. His left eye squinted like mine did ever since the time a folding machine in the box factory recoiled into my brow, sending me to the hospital. The girl's mouth dropped as the swizzle male's head separated from the torso and floated up.

"I'm so sorry," she said, and then I saw her fingers, long like mine.

"I'm so sorry," Frances—her mother?—added.

The entire body was floating now, in ten or so pieces. Random bubbles shoved it one way, then another. Brownian motion, I recalled from school physics. Statistics. No specific cause, just like Dad always said. I nodded, and I stood. It was time to head for Joe's. No time to finish even my fifty-eight-year-old wine.

It was a lousy vintage anyway.

photo: Emily Mills

Masques for the Fields of Time is Joe Taylor's fourth story collection. He lives in the backwoods of Alabama, where there are no pro-sports teams or television stations. O wondrous land!